INDIAN PRIME MINISTERS

WITH NOTABLE SPEECHES

Dr. Gagan Jain, *D.Litt.*

MGL®

NEW DELHI (INDIA)

INDIAN PRIME MINISTERS

WITH NOTABLE SPEECHES

This English Edition, Published in India

Published by

MG BOOKS

An Imprint of

MAANU GRAPHICS

(PUBLISHERS OF GENERAL BOOKS)

5FF, Ganpati Bhawan, 21 Ansari Road,
Darya Ganj, New Delhi-110002
Ph: 43755225, 9315898404
E-mail : maanugraphics@yahoo.com
mgbooks.maanu@yahoo.com

Printed at

Satyam Enterprises, Delhi

CONTENTS

INTRODUCTION

PRIME MINISTERS OF INDIA
APPOINTMENT, FUNCTIONS & TENURE

The Prime Minister of India is, in practice, the most powerful person in the Government of India. The Prime Minister is technically outranked by the head of state, the President of India. But, as is typical in most parliamentary democracies, because the head of state's duties are largely ceremonial, the Prime Minister is the head of government and has effective responsibility for executive power.

The Prime Minister is generally the leader of a party (or coalition of parties) that has a majority in the Lok Sabha, the lower house of the Parliament of India. The Prime Minister either has to be a current member of one of the houses of Parliament, or be elected within six months of being appointed.

Formally, the Prime Minister is appointed by the President. The President is expected to invite that person to be the Prime Minister who has been elected the leader of the parliamentary party that commands an absolute majority in the Lok Sabha. But when no single party enjoys a majority, the president has some discretion: he or she may invite the leader of a combination of parties constituting the majority in the Lok Sabha or the leader of the single largest party in the Lok Sabha.

The Prime Minister selects the members of the Council of Ministers who are formally appointed by the President. He allocates portfolios among the ministers and he can drop any minister. The Prime Minister presides over the meetings of the Council of Ministers. He decides the policies of the government. He coordinates the work of different ministries and solves inter - departmental conflicts. The Prime Minister is the Chairperson of the Planning Commission which is a key body in the process of planning.

The Prime Minister advises the President on all important matters like appointments judges of the High Courts and the Supreme Court, Chief Election Commissioner, Comptroller and Auditor General. He also advises the President on the summoning and proroguing of the Parliament, the dissolving of the Lok Sabha and the declaration of emergencies.

He is a link between the President and the Cabinet. Fourteen individuals have served as Prime Minister of India. Jawaharlal Nehru served for four consecutive terms (1947-1952, 1952-1957, 1957-1962, and 1962-1964). Indira Gandhi served three times (1966-1971, 1971-1977, and 1980-1984), and Atal Behari Vajpayee served on three occasions (1996, 1998-1999, 1999-2004). Gulzari Lal Nanda served as acting Prime Minister during two transition periods.

The early years were dominated by the Indian National Congress party, which held the premiership for the first thirty years of India's independence. Morarji Desai became the first non-Congress Prime Minister in 1977, representing the broad Janata coalition. In December 1989 V P Singh of that coalition's successor, the Janata Dal, became the first prime minister of that party. In 1996, Atal Behari Vajpayee of the Bharatiya Janata Party became the first person from that party to become Prime Minister. He was again returned to power in 1998 and in 1999. The 2004 elections to the Lok Sabha restored Congress to power, and Dr. Manmohan Singh was named the Prime Minister-designate on 19 May 2004. He was sworn in on May 22, 2004. Singh is the first Sikh Prime Minister of India. He is also the only Prime Minister who has never been elected to the Lok Sabha.

The official residence of the Prime Minister of India is 7 Race Course Road. Some prime ministers have chosen to use part of their official residence as their office too, in other words, 7 RCR has functioned as the PMO (Prime Minister's Office) on several occasion in the past. The incumbent prime minister, Dr. Manmohan Singh's PMO is located at South Block and not at 7 RCR.

26th January, 2008 ***—Author***

THE PRIME MINISTERS OF INDIA

— **Shri Jawaharlal Nehru**
August 15, 1947 - May 27, 1964
Congress

— **Shri Gulzari Lal Nanda**
May 27, 1964 - June 9, 1964
Congress

— **Shri Lal Bahadur Shastri**
June 9, 1964 - January 11, 1966
Congress

— **Shri Gulzari Lal Nanda**
January 11, 1966 - January 24, 1966
Congress

— **Mrs. Indira Gandhi**
January 24, 1966 - March 24, 1977
Congress

— **Shri Morarji Desai**
March 24, 1977 - July 28, 1979
Janata Party

— **Shri Charan Singh**
July 28, 1979 - January 14, 1980
Janata Party

— **Mrs. Indira Gandhi**
January 14, 1980 - October 31, 1984
Congress (I)

— **Shri Rajiv Gandhi**
October 31, 1984 - December 2, 1989
Congress (I)

— **Shri Vishwanath Pratap Singh**
December 2, 1989 - November 10, 1990
Janata Dal

— **Shri Chandra Shekhar**
November 10, 1990 - June 21, 1991
Janata Dal (S)

— **Shri P. V. Narasimha Rao**
June 21, 1991- May 16, 1996
Congress (I)

— **Shri Atal Bihari Vajpayee**
May 16, 1996 - June 1, 1996
Bharatiya Janata Party

— **Shri H. D. Deve Gowda**
June 1, 1996 - April 21, 1997
Janata Dal

— **Shri Inder Kumar Gujral**
April 21, 1997 - March 19, 1998
Janata Dal

— **Shri Atal Bihari Vajpayee**
March 19, 1998 - May 22, 2004
Bharatiya Janata Party

— **Dr. Manmohan Singh**
May 22, 2004 - May 26, 2014
Indian National Congress

— **Shri Narendra Damodardas Modi**
May 26, 2014 - till date
Bharatiya Janata Party

JAWAHARLAL NEHRU

SHRI JAWAHARLAL NEHRU (1889-1964), India's first prime minister, was the chief architect of domestic and foreign policies between 1947 and 1964. Pt. Jawaharlal Nehru was born in Allabahad on November 14, 1889. He received his early education at home under private tutors. At the age of fifteen, he went to England and after two years at Harrow, joined Cambridge University where he took his tripos in Natural Sciences. He was later called to the Bar from Inner

Temple. He returned to India in 1912 and plunged straight into politics. Even as a student, he had been interested in the struggle of all nations who suffered under foreign domination. He took keen interest in the Sinn Fein Movement in Ireland. In India, he was inevitably drawn into the struggle for independence.

In 1912, he attended the Bankipore Congress as a delegate, and became Secretary of the Home Rule League, Allahabad in 1919. In 1916 he had his first meeting with Mahatma Gandhi and felt immensely inspired by him. He organised the first Kisan March in Pratapgarh District of Uttar Pradesh in 1920. He was twice imprisoned in connection with the Non-Cooperation Movement of 1920-22.

Pt. Nehru became the General Secretary of the All India Congress Committee in September 1923. He toured Italy, Switzerland, England, Belgium, Germany and Russia in 1926. In Belgium, he attended the Congress of Oppressed Nationalities in Brussels as an official delegate of the Indian National Congress. He also attended the tenth anniversary celebrations of the October Socialist Revolution in Moscow in 1927. Earlier, in 1926, at the Madras Congress, Nehru had been instrumental in committing the Congress to the goal of Independence. While leading a procession against the Simon commission, he was lathi-charged in Lucknow in 1928. On August 29, 1928 he attended the All-Party Congress and was one of the signatories to the Nehru Report on Indian Constitutional Reform, named after his father Shri Motilal Nehru. The same year, he also founded the 'Independence for India League', which advocated complete severance of the British connection with India, and became its General Secretary.

In 1929, Pt. Nehru was elected President of the Lahore Session of the Indian National Congress, where complete independence for the country was adopted as the goal. He was imprisoned several times during 1930-35 in connection with the Salt Satyagraha and other movements launched by the Congress. He completed his 'Autobiography' in Almora Jail on February 14, 1935. After release, he flew to Switzerland to see his ailing wife and visited London in February-March, 1936. He also visited Spain in July 1938, when the country was in the throws of Civil War. Just before the court-break of the Second World War, he visited China too.

On October 31, 1940 Pt. Nehru was arrested for offering individual Satyagraha to protest against India's forced participation in war. He was released along with the other leaders in December 1941. On August 7, 1942 Pt. Nehru moved the historic 'Quit India' resolution at the A.I.C.C. session in Bombay. On August 8,1942 he was arrested along with other leaders and taken to Ahmednagar Fort. This was his longest and also his last detention. In all, he suffered imprisonment nine times. After his release in January 1945, he organized legal defence for those officers and men of the INA charged with treason. In March 1946, Pt. Nehru toured South East Asia. He was elected President of the Congress for the fourth time on July 6, 1946 and again for three more terms from 1951 to 1954.

Nehru's appreciation for parliamentary democracy coupled with concerns for the poor and underprivileged enabled him to formulate policies that often reflected his socialist leanings. Both as prime minister and as Congress president, Nehru pushed through the Indian Parliament, dominated by members of his own party, a series of legal reforms intended to emancipate Hindu women and bring equality. These reforms included raising the minimum marriageable age from twelve to fifteen, empowering women to divorce their husbands and inherit property, and declaring illegal the ruinous dowry system.

The threat of escalating violence and the potential for "red revolution" across the country seemed daunting in the face of the country's growing population, unemployment, and economic inequality. Jawaharlal Nehru induced Parliament to pass a number of laws abolishing absentee landlordism and conferring titles to land on the actual cultivators who could document their right to occupancy. Under his direction, the central Planning Commission allocated resources to heavy industries, such as steel plants and hydroelectric projects, and to revitalizing cottage industries. Whether producing sophisticated defense matériel or manufacturing everyday consumer goods, industrial complexes emerged across the country, accompanied by the expansion of scientific research and teaching at universities, institutes of technology, and research centers.

Jawaharlal Nehru demonstrated tremendous enthusiasm for India's moral leadership, especially among the newly independent Asian and African nations, in a world polarized by Cold War ideology and threatened by nuclear weapons. His guiding principles were nationalism, anticolonialism, internationalism, and nonalignment. He attained international prestige during his first decade in office, but after the Soviet invasion of Hungary in 1956—when New Delhi tilted toward Moscow—criticisms grew against his inconsistency in condemning Western but not communist aggression. In dealing with Pakistan, Nehru failed to formulate a consistent policy and was critical of the improving ties between Pakistan and the United States; mutual hostility and suspicion persisted as a result. Despite attempts at improving relations with China, based on his much-publicized five principles—territorial integrity and sovereignty, nonaggression, noninterference, equality and cooperation, and peaceful coexistence—war with China erupted in 1962. The war was a rude awakening for Nehru, as India proved ill-equipped and unprepared to defend its northern borders. At the conclusion of the conflict, the Chinese forces were partially withdrawn and an unofficial demilitarized zone was established, but India's prestige and self-esteem had suffered. Physically debilitated and mentally exhausted, Nehru suffered a stroke and died in office in May 1964. Jawaharlal Nehru's legacy of a democratic, federal, and secular India continues to survive in spite of attempts by later leaders to establish either an autocratic or a theocratic state.

SPEECH ON THE GRANTING OF INDIAN INDEPENDENCE, AUGUST 14, 1947

Long years ago we made a tryst with destiny, and now the time comes when we shall redeem our pledge, not wholly or in full measure, but very substantially. At the stroke of the midnight hour, when the world sleeps, India will awake to life and freedom. A moment comes, which comes but rarely in history, when we step out from the old to the new, when an age ends, and when the soul of a nation, long supressed, finds utterance. It is fitting that at this solemn moment we take the pledge of dedication to the service of Inida and her people and to the still larger cause of humanity.

At the dawn of history India started on her unending quest, and trackless centuries are filled with her striving and the grandeur of her success and her failures. Through good and ill fortune alike she has never lost sight of that quest or forgotten the ideals which gave her strength. We end today a period of ill fortune and India discovers herself again. The achievement we celebrate today is but a step, an opening of opportunity, to the greater triumphs and achievements that await us. Are we brave enough and wise enough to grasp this opportunity and accept the challenge of the future?

Freedom and power bring responsibility. The responsibility rests upon this Assembly, a sovereign body representing the sovereign people of India. Before the birth of freedom we have endured all the pains of labour and our hearts are heavy with the memory of this sorrow. Some of those pains continue even now. Nevertheless, the past is over and it is the future that beckons to us now.

That future is not one of ease or resting but of incessant striving so that we may fulfil the pledges we have so often taken and the one we shall take today. The service of India means the service of the millions who suffer. It means the ending of poverty and ignorance and disease and inequality of opportunity. The ambition of the greatest man of our generation has been to wipe every tear from every eye. That may be beyond us, but as long as there are tears and suffering, so long our work will not be over.

And so we have to labour and to work, and work hard, to give reality to our dreams. Those dreams are for India, but they are also for the world, for all the nations and peoples are too closely knit together today for any one of them to imagine that it can live apart Peace has been said to be indivisible; so is freedom, so is prosperity now, and so also is disaster in this One World that can no longer be split into isolated fragments.

To the people of India, whose representatives we are, we make an appeal to join us with faith and confidence in this great adventure. This is no time for petty and destructive criticism, no time for ill-will or blaming others. We have to build the noble mansion of free India where all her children may dwell.

SPEECH BEFORE A JOURNALISTS MEETING ON AUGUST 15, 1947

THE appointed day has come-the day appointed by destiny-and India stands forth again, after long slumber and struggle, awake, vital, free and independent. The past clings on to us still in some measure and we have to do much before we redeem the pledges we have so often taken. Yet the turning-point is past, and history begins anew for us, the history which we shall live and act and others will write about.

It is a fateful moment for us in India, for all Asia and for the world. A new star rises, the star of freedom in the East, a new hope comes into being, a vision long cherished materializes. May the star never set and that hope never be betrayed!

We rejoice in that freedom, even though clouds surround us, and many of our people are sorrowstricken and difficult problems encompass us. But freedom brings responsibilities and burdens and we have to face them in the spirit of a free and disciplined people.

On this day our first thoughts go to the architect of this freedom, the Father of our Nation [Gandhi], who, embodying the old spirit of India, held aloft the torch of freedom and lighted up the darkness that surrounded us. We have often been unworthy followers of his and have strayed from his message, but not only we but succeeding generations will remember this message and bear the imprint in their hearts of this great son of India, magnificent in his faith and strength and courage and humility. We shall never allow that torch of freedom to be blown out, however high the wind or stormy the tempest.

Our next thoughts must be of the unknown volunteers and soldiers of freedom who, without praise or reward, have served India even unto death.

We think also of our brothers and sisters who have been cut off from us by political boundaries and who unhappily cannot share at present in the freedom that has come. They are of us and will remain of us whatever may happen, and we shall be sharers in their good [or] ill fortune alike.

The future beckons to us. Whither do we go and what shall be our endeavour? To bring freedom and opportunity to the common man, to the peasants and workers of India; to fight and end poverty and ignorance and disease; to build up a prosperous, democratic and progressive nation, and to create social, economic and political institutions which will ensure justice and fullness of life to every man and woman.

We have hard work ahead. There is no resting for any one of us till we redeem our pledge in full, till we make all the people of India what destiny intended them to be. We are citizens of a great country on the verge of bold advance, and we have to live up to that high standard. All of us, to whatever religion we may belong, are equally the children of India with equal rights, privileges and obligations. We cannot encourage communalism or narrow-mindedness, for no nation can be great whose people are narrow in thought or in action.

To the nations and peoples of the world we send greetings and pledge ourselves to cooperate with them in furthering peace, freedom and democracy.

And to India, our much-loved motherland, the ancient, the eternal and the ever-new, we pay our reverent homage and we bind ourselves afresh to her service.

JAI HIND.

AT THE UNITED NATIONS GENERAL ASSEMBLY, PARIS, NOVEMBER 3, 1948.

I COME from a country which, after a long struggle, though that struggle was a peaceful struggle, attained its freedom and its independence. In these long years of struggle we were taught by our great leader never to forget not only the objectives we had, but also the methods whereby we should achieve those objectives. Always he laid stress on this, that it was not good enough to have a good objective, that it was equally important that the means of attaining those objectives were good, means were always as important as ends. You will permit me to repeat that here, because I am convinced that, however good the ends, the larger ends of the United Nations, or the lesser objectives which we may from time to time have before us either as individual nations or as groups of nations, it is important that we should remember that the best of objectives may not be reached if our eyes are bloodshot and our minds clouded with passion.

Therefore, it becomes essential for us, for a while, to think more of how we are doing things than what we are aiming at, even though we should never forget what we are aiming at. It becomes necessary for us always to remember the principles and the purposes for which this great Assembly was formed.

Now, a mere repetition of those principles and purposes would perhaps indicate to us how sometimes, with passion and prejudice, we swerve away from that path. This Assembly took shape after two mighty wars and as a consequence of those wars. What has been the lesson of those wars? Surely the lesson of those wars has been that out of hatred and violence you will not build peace. It is a contradiction in terms. The lesson of history, the long course of history, and more especially the lesson of the last great wars which have devastated humanity, has been that out of hatred and violence only hatred and violence will come. We have got into a cycle of hatred and violence, and not the most brilliant debate will get us out of It, unless we look some other way and find some other means. It is obvious that if we continue in this cycle and have wars which this Assembly was especially meant to avoid and prevent, the result will not only be tremendous devastation all over the world, but non-achievement by any individual power or group of its objective.

It may be that it is difficult to get this hatred and prejudice and fear out of our minds. Nevertheless, unless we try to proceed in this way, to cast out this fear, we shall never succeed. Of that I am quite convinced.

I feel that today the world is tied up in fears and apprehensions, some of them justified, no doubt. But where a person feels fear, bad consequences and evil consequences follow. Fear is not a good companion. It is surprising to see that this sense of fear is pervading great countries fear, and grave fear of war, and fear of many things. I think that it is admitted, or it will be admitted, that no aggression of any kind can be tolerated, because the very idea of aggression must upset the balance and lead to conflict. Aggression of every type must be resisted. In existing circumstances it is difficult for people to say that they will not defend themselves, because if there is fear of aggression one has to defend oneself against aggression. We have to defend ourselves, but even in defending ourselves, we must not submit ourselves to this Assembly without clean hands.

I have no doubt that this Assembly is going to solve our problems. I am not afraid of the future. I have no fear in my mind, and I have no fear, even though India, from a military point of view, is of no great consequence. I am not afraid of the bigness of great powers, and their armies, their fleets and their atom bombs. That is the lesson which my Master taught me. We stood as an unarmed people against a great country and a powerful empire.

We were supported and strengthened, because throughout all this period we decided not to submit to evil, and I think that is the lesson which I have before me and which is before us today. I do not know if it is possible to apply this to the problems which face the world today. It is a terrible problem, but I think if we banish this fear, if we have confidence, even though we may take risks of trust rather than risk violent language, violent actions and in the end war, I think those risks are worth taking.

However, we do not think that the problems of the world or of India can be solved by thinking in terms of aggression or war or violence. We are frail mortals, and we cannot always live up to the teaching of the great man who led our nation to freedom. But that lesson has sunk deep into our souls and, so long as we remember it, I am sure we shall be on the right path. And, if I may venture to suggest this to the General Assembly, I think that if the essentials of that lesson are kept in mind, perhaps our approach to the problems of today will be different: perhaps the conflicts that always hang over us will appear a little less deep than they are and in fact gradually fade away.

I should like to state to this General Assembly, on behalf of my people and my Government, that we adhere completely and absolutely to the principles and purposes of the United Nations Charter and that we shall try, to the best of our ability. to work for the realisation of those principles and purposes.

AT THE UNITED NATIONS OF GENERAL ASSEMBLY, NEW YORK, NOVEMBER 10, 1961

We talk about many problems like disarmament, and sometimes one has the feeling that although there is apparent agreement, really behind it there is not that faith in disarmament that is necessary, and that talks are more of some kind of attempt to put the other party in the wrong rather than to achieve something, while it is of the utmost importance that achievement should take place. I am convinced that the modern world cannot continue for long without full. disarmament. All these problems have come up again and again. Ultimately it is perhaps true that the material advance which has taken place in the world, and that is magnificent, has gone far ahead of the development of human minds, which lag behind. They do not fit in with the modem age, and the mind still thinks in its narrow terms of 100 to 200 years ago of how nations function, how diplomats function and how wars took place.

We know, we have heard and we have read about the new possibility of a nuclear war. Nevertheless, emotionally, we do not understand it fully. Otherwise it seems to me impossible why there should be these continuing deadlocks and impasses because the fact is that under modem conditions war must be ruled out or the world of civilisation or humanity has to submit to the ending of all it has laboured for thousands of years. if that is true, then surely it is important and urgent that we should approach this question with speed, deliberation and a determination to solve it rather than merely show that the other party is wrong.

I mentioned disarmament. This Assembly last year, I think decided almost unanimously in favour of general. widespread disarmament. The great nations of the world have all committed themselves to that. The United States, through its President, recently put forward proposals which are in line with what this Assembly has decided. The Soviet Union has put forward proposals to the same effect, varying slightly but essentially aiming at the same thing. Even in broad outline there is a good deal of commonness about them. If that is so, what comes in our way, why should we not grasp this opportunity when there is so much agreement and remove this fear and terror from people's minds and devote all the great energies and resources of the people to world advancement. I do not know except what I have said, that we are quite unable to get out Of old ways of thinking which ought to have no place in the modern world, old ways of hatred and violence of yesterday but a violence which could exterminate all of us, not realizing that there is no victory today for any country in a major war - only defeat and extermination for all. If that is so, then surely this major and outstanding question must be dealt with speed and those great countries, especially those which have the greatest responsibility because they possess the biggest weapons of warfare - nuclear weapons - should address themselves again and again to negotiations, to talks, to the consideration of this problem together to find some remedy, with the determination that they will not separate until they have come to some agreements, of course. Those agreements cannot be merely agreements of some countries, however great. They must represent all the members of this United Nations in this great body. But I do think that it is better for those countries - a few of them - to deal with this problem rather than for a larger body to deal with it to begin with. I feel rather strongly on this question although we in India are not situated in the major theatres of a possible war - probably not. Nevertheless, I feel that everything that man has striven for in the past thousands of years is at stake today. As strongly as I feel about these colonial matters, about the freedom of colonial countries and others, I do think that the major question and the biggest question of war and peace and disarmament. There is no conflict between those.

In fact, the whole atmosphere of the world will change if disarmament comes in and these present problems go towards solution. How then are we to do it? I do not know. The president was good enough the East or to my wisdom. It was kind of him to make that reference to me, but I possess no greater wisdom than each one of us here. Only perhaps in some matters, some of us may feel a little more, some of us who have experienced many ups and downs in their lives may think more deeply about them. But It is wisdom that we want, it Is the common wisdom that should come to everyone. It is no mystery. In the problems before us there are no mysteries. They are obvious problems, and the fear of war is obvious. The fear that grips mankind is obvious. How can we go on dealing with the secondary questions of the world, discussing them, etc., when this basic problem deludes us? As a part of this question of disarmament there is the particular question today of nuclear tests. The General Assembly passed a resolution recently about them. It was, I think, a great misfortune that after a period of abstinence from nuclear tests there was resumption. There can be no doubt that that turned the attention of the world in a wrong direction, apart from the harm it might do. Immediately the idea of a possible war became more prevalent. Immediately it became more difficult to have treaties for ending nuclear tests because while treaties are essential, are necessary for this. when the whole atmosphere becomes one of fear and apprehension, it becomes more difficult to get a treaty. I do think, and I would beg the countries concerned to realize, that they are doing a grave disservice to the world, to their countries even, by not putting an end to this business of nuclear tests by a treaty as rapidly as possible.

The Assembly has passed a resolution in favour of some kind of moratorium. No one imagines that a voluntary moratorium is going to solve this question. There must be stricter controls by treaty and otherwise. But while that should be aimed at and worked for and achieved as rapidly as possible, one should not leave the door open, while you discuss It, for these nuclear tests, to go on. Arguments may be raised that one party or one country gets an advantage over the other and these arguments may have substances. yet my own reaction to these nuclear tests is a very strong one. I think they are basically evil. They encourage evil. Therefore, the sooner this evil is dealt with the better.

GULZARI LAL NANDA

SHRI GULZARILAL NANDA was born on July 4, 1898, in Sialkot in the Undivided Punjab, now in Punjab, Pakistan. He was educated at *Lahore*, *Agra* and *Allahabad*. He worked as a research scholar on labour problems at Allahabad University (1920-1921) and became Professor of Economics at the National College (Bombay) in 1921. He joined the Non-Cooperation Movement during the same year. In 1922, he become Secretary of the Ahmedabad Textile Labour Association in which he worked until 1946. He was imprisoned for Satyagraha in 1932, and again from 1942 to 1944.

Shri Nanda was elected to the Bombay Legislative Assembly in 1937 and was Parliamentary Secretary (Labour and Excise) to the Government of Bombay from 1937 to 1939. Later, as Labour Minister of the Bombay Government (1946-50), he successfully piloted the Labour Disputes Bill in the State Assembly. He served as Trustee, Kasturba Memorial Trust; Secretary, Hindustan Mazdoor Sevak Sangh; and Chairman, Bombay Housing Board. He was also a Member of the National Planning Committee. He was largely instrumental in organising the Indian National Trade Union Congress and later became its President.

In 1947, he went to Geneva as a Government delegate to the International Labour Conference. He worked on the 'The Freedom of Association Committee' appointed by the Conference and visited Sweden, France, Switzerland, Belgium and England to study labour and housing conditions in those countries.

In March 1950, he joined the Planning Commission as its Vice-Chairman. In September the following year, he was appointed Planning Minister in the Union Government. In addition, he was also given charge of the portfolios of Irrigation and Power. He was elected to the House of the People from Bombay in the general elections of 1952 and was re-appointed Minister for Planning Irrigation and Power. He led the Indian Delegation to the Plan Consultative Committee held at Singapore in 1955, and the International Labour Conference held at Geneva in 1959.

Shri Nanda was elected to the Lok Sabha in the 1957 general elections, and was appointed Union Minister for Labour and Employment and Planning and, later, as Deputy Chairman of the Planning Commission. He visited the Federal Republic of Germany Yugoslavia and Austria in 1959.

He was re-elected to the Lok Sabha in the 1962 general elections from Sabarkantha Constituency in Gujarat. He initiated the Congress Forum for Socialist Action in 1962. He was Union Minister for Labour and Employment in 1962 and 1963 and Minister for Home Affairs from 1963 to 1966.

Following the death of Pt. Nehru, he was a sworn in as Interim Prime Minister of India on May 27, 1964. Again on January 11, 1966, he was sworn in as Prime Minister following the death of Shri Lal Bahadur Shastri at Tashkent.

Nanda died on 15 January 1998 at the age of 99.

LAL BAHADUR SHASTRI

SHRI LAL BAHADUR SHASTRI became the second Prime Minister of India after the death of Jawaharlal Nehru on 27 May 1964. He served the nation as Prime Minister for 19 months and two days i.e. from 9 June 1964 to 11 January 1966, at a very crucial period of independent India.

Lal Bahadur was born on 2 October, 1904 in Mughalsarai, Uttar Pradesh as Lal Bahadur Srivastava. His father Sharada Prasad was a poor school teacher, who later became a clerk in the Revenue Office at Allahabad. When Lal Bahadur was three months old, he slipped out of his mother's arms into a cowherd's basket at the ghats of the Ganges. The cowherd, who had no children, took the child as a gift from God and took him home. Lal Bahadur's parents lodged a complaint with the police, who traced the child, and returned him to his parents.

Lal Bahadur's father died when he was only a year and a half old. His mother Ramdulari Devi took him and his two sisters to her father's house and settled down there. Lal Bahadur stayed at his grandfather Hazari Lal's house till he was ten. Since there was no high school in their town, he was sent to Varanasi where he stayed with his maternal uncle and joined the Harischandra High School. While in Varanasi, Shastri once went with his friends to see a fair on the other bank of the Ganges. On the way back he had no money for the boat fare. Instead of borrowing from his friends, he jumped into the river and swam to the other bank.

As a boy, Lal Bahadur loved reading books and was fond of Guru Nanak's verses. He revered Bal Gangadhar Tilak, the Indian nationalist, social reformer and freedom fighter. After hearing a speech of Mahatma Gandhi at Varanasi in 1915, he dedicated his life to the service of the country. He also dropped his surname, as it indicated his caste and he was against the caste system. During the non-cooperation movement of Mahatma Gandhi in 1921, he joined processions in defiance of the prohibitory order. He was arrested but let off as he was a minor. He then enrolled at the nationalist Kashi Vidyapeeth in Varanasi. During his four years there, he was greatly influenced by the lectures of Dr. Bhagawandas on philosophy. Upon completion of his course at Kashi Vidyapeeth in 1926, he was given the title *Shastri* ("Scholar"). The title was a bachelor's degree awarded by the Vidya Peeth, but it stuck as part of his name. He also enrolled himself as a life member of the Servants of the People Society and began to work for the upliftment of the Harijans at Muzaffarpur. Later he became the President of the Society.

In 1927, Shastri married Lalita Devi of Mirzapur. In spite of the prevailing hefty dowry tradition, Shastri accepted only a *charkha* and a few yards of *khadi* as dowry. In 1930, he threw himself into the freedom struggle during Mahatma Gandhi's Salt Satyagraha. He was imprisoned for two and a half years. Once, while he was in prison, one of his daughters fell seriously ill. He was released for fifteen days, on the condition that he not take part in the freedom movement. However, his daughter died before he reached home. After performing the funeral rites, he voluntarily returned to prison, even before the expiry of the period. A year later, he asked for permission to go home for a week, as his son had contracted influenza. The permission was given, but his son's illness was not cured in a week. In spite of his family's pleadings, he kept his promise to the jail officers and returned to the prison.

Later, he worked as the Organizing Secretary of the Parliamentary Board of U.P. in 1937. In 1940, he was sent to prison for one year, for offering individual Satyagraha to support the freedom movement. On August 8, 1942, Mahatma Gandhi issued the Quit India speech at Gowalia Tank in Mumbai, demanding that the British leave India. Shastri, who had just then come out after a year in prison, traveled to Allahabad. For a week, he sent instructions to the freedom fighters from Jawaharlal Nehru's home, Anand Bhavan. A few days later, he was arrested and imprisoned until 1946. Shastri spent almost nine years in jail in total. During his stay in prison, he spent time reading books and became familiar with the works of western philosophers, revolutionaries and social reformers. He also translated the autobiography of Madam Curie into Hindi language.

Following India's independence, Shastri was appointed Parliamentary Secretary in his home state, Uttar Pradesh. He became the Minister of Police and Transport under Govind Ballabh Pant's Chief Ministership. As the Transport Minister, he was the first to appoint women conductors. As the minister in charge of the Police Department, he ordered that Police use jets of water instead of lathis to disperse unruly crowds.

In 1951, he was made the General Secretary of the All-India Congress Committee, with Jawaharlal Nehru as the President. He was directly responsible for the selection of candidates and the direction of publicity and electioneering activities. He played an important role in the landslide successes of the Congress Party in the Indian General Elections of 1952, 1957 and 1962.

In 1951, Nehru nominated him to the Rajya Sabha. He served as the Minister of Railways and Transport in the Central Cabinet from 1951 to 1956. In 1956, he offered his resignation after a railway accident at Mahbubnagar led to 112 deaths. However, Nehru did not accept his resignation. Three months later, he resigned accepting moral and constitutional responsibility for a railway accident at Ariyalur in Tamil Nadu that resulted in 144 deaths. While speaking in the Parliament on the incident, the then Prime Minister, Jawaharlal Nehru, stated that he was accepting the resignation because it would set an example in constitutional propriety and not because Shastri was in any way responsible for the accident. Shastri's unprecedented gesture was greatly appreciated by the citizens.

In 1957, Shastri returned to the Cabinet following the General Elections, first as the Minister for Transport and Communications, and then as the Minister of Commerce and Industry. In 1961, he became Minister for Home. As Union Home Minister he was instrumental in appointing the Committee on Prevention of Corruption under the Chairmanship of K. Santhanam.

Jawaharlal Nehru died in office on May 27, 1964 and left a vacuum. The then Congress Party President K. Kamaraj was instrumental in making Shastri as Prime Minister on June 9. Shastri, though mild-mannered and soft-spoken, was a Nehruvian socialist and thus held appeal to those wishing to prevent the ascent of conservative right-winger Morarji Desai.

In his first broadcast as Prime Minister, on June 11, 1964, Shastri stated:

"There comes a time in the life of every nation when it stands at the cross-roads of history and must choose which way to go. But for us there need be no difficulty or hesitation, no looking to right or left. Our way is straight and clear – the building up of a socialist democracy at home with freedom and prosperity for all, and the maintenance of world peace and friendship with all nations."

Shastri worked by his natural characteristics to obtain compromises between opposing viewpoints, but in his short tenure was ineffectual in dealing with the economic crisis and food shortage in the nation. However, he commanded a great deal of respect in the Indian populace, and he used it to advantage in pushing the Green Revolution in India; which directly led to India becoming a food-surplus nation, although he did not live to see it. During the 22-day war with Pakistan,

Lal Bahadur Shastri created the slogan of "Jai Jawan Jai Kisan", underlining the need to boost India's food production. Apart from emphasizing the Green Revolution, he was instrumental in promoting the White Revolution. Greatly impressed by a visit to the Kaira district in October 1964, he urged the rest of the country to learn from the successful experiment at Anand. The National Dairy Development Board was formed in 1965 during his tenure as Prime Minister.

Though he was Socialist, Shastri stated that India cannot have a regimented type of economy. During his tenure as Prime Minister, he visited Russia, Yugoslavia, England, Canada and Burma in 1965.

Indo-Pakistani War of 1965 The chief problem for Shastri's administration was Pakistan. Laying claim to half of the Kutch peninsula, Pakistan sent incursion forces in August 1965, which skirmished with Indian tank divisions. In his report to the Lok Sabha on the confrontation in Kutch, Shastri stated:

"In the utilization of our limited resources, we have always given primacy to plans and projects for economic development. It would, therefore, be obvious for anyone who is prepared to look at things objectively that India can have no possible interest in provoking border incidents or in building up an atmosphere of strife... In these circumstances, the duty of Government is quite clear and this duty will be discharged fully and effectively... We would prefer to live in poverty for as long as necessary but we shall not allow our freedom to be subverted."

Under a scheme proposed by the British PM, Pakistan obtained 10%, in place of their original claim of 50% of the territory. But Pakistan's aggressive intentions were also focused on Kashmir. When armed infiltrators from Pakistan began entering the State of Jammu and Kashmir, Shastri made it clear to Pakistan that force would be met with force. Just in September 1965, major incursions of militants and Pakistani soldiers began, hoping not only to break-down the government but incite a sympathetic revolt. The revolt did not happen, and India sent its forces across the Ceasefire Line (now Line of Control) and threatened Pakistan by crossing the International Border near Lahore as war broke out on a general scale. Massive tank battles occurred in the Punjab, and while Pakistani forces made some gains, Indian forces captured the key post at Haji Pir, in Kashmir, and brought the Pakistani city of Lahore under artillery and mortar fire.

On 17 September 1965, while the Indo-Pak war was on, India received a letter from China. In the letter, China alleged that the Indian army had set up army equipment in Chinese territory, and India would face China's wrath, unless the equipments are pulled down. In spite of the threat of aggression from China, Shastri declared "China's allegation is untrue. If China attacks India it is our firm resolve to fight for our freedom. The might of China will not deter us from defending our territorial integrity.". The Chinese did not respond, but the Indo-Pak war resulted in great personnel and material casualties for both Pakistan and India.

The Indo-Pak war ended on September 23, 1965 with a United Nations-mandated ceasefire. In a broadcast to the nation on the day the of ceasefire, Shastri stated:

"While the conflict between the armed forces of the two countries has come to an end, the more important thing for the United Nations and all those who stand for peace is to bring to an end the deeper conflict... How can this be brought about? In our view, the only answer lies in peaceful coexistence. India has stood for the principle of coexistence and championed it all over the world. Peaceful coexistence is possible among nations no matter how deep the differences between them, how far apart they are in their political and economic systems, no matter how intense the issues that divide them."

After the declaration of ceasefire, Shastri and Pakistani President Muhammad Ayub Khan attended a summit in Tashkent (former USSR, now in modern Uzbekistan), organised by Kosygin. On January 10, 1966, Shastri and Khan signed the Tashkent Declaration. Shastri died in Tashkent, Uzbekistan (then Soviet Union) on 11 January 1966, one day after signing a peace treaty to end the 1965 Indo-Pakistan War. He is the only Indian Prime Minister, and indeed probably one of the few heads of government, to have died in office overseas. Some conspiracy theories allege his death to be of unnatural causes.

The news of Lal Bahadur Shastri's death struck India like a bolt from the blue. The entire nation was plunged in grief. Some people suspected foulplay also. Gone was the war hero and the messenger of peace, gone was the great statesman who restored to India her honor and self- respect in the assembly of nations.

All his lifetime, Shastri was known for honesty and humility. He was the first person to be posthumously awarded the Bharat Ratna, and a memorial "Vijay Ghat" was built for him in Delhi. Several educational institutes, roads, public squares and monuments in India are named after him. The Lal Bahadur Shastri Stadium in Hyderabad, Andhra Pradesh is an example.

In 2005, the Government of India opened the Lal Bahadur Shastri Memorial and set up a library in New Delhi, as part of the Lal Bahadur Shastri Centenary Celebrations. Doordarshan produced a docu-drama on his life, and a national award was instituted in his name. Also, a chair was created in his name in the field of democracy and governance in Delhi University.

EXCERPTS FROM HIS REPLY TO THE DEBATE ON THE MOTION OF THANKS FOR THE PRESIDENT'S ADDRESS IN THE RAJYA SABHA ON MARCH 9, 1965.

Vital Issues

THERE has been a prolonged discussion on the President's Address and except perhaps for a couple of very critical speeches, on the whole I must say that they were set in the proper key. The most important problem before us today is the economic development of our country, and we have naturally to concentrate our utmost attention on that problem. Sometimes an impression is given that there is no progress or no adequate development in the economic field. I would not go into the past history but during the last decade or twelve years, we have touched almost every vital item of industry. The essential ingredients of industry like oil, mines and minerals, steel, power, all these items have been not only fully explored but after giving some time to the exploration part of it, the Government has made definite progress and the industrial production has considerably gone up. There have been bottlenecks in the development of cement and steel. I might say that cement production during the next twelve months is expected to increase by about I million tonnes. Steel production between this year and the next two is expected to increase by 1/2 million tonnes. Fertilizer output is also expected to go up by 100,000 tonnes with the Trombay fertiliser plant going into production.

Then in regard to power, there will be an increase of nearly 3 million kilowatts in the power generating capacity of the country. In regard to steel, we have signed the Bokaro agreement. Two additional blast furnaces are being constructed at Bhilai in respect of steel plant expansion in the Fourth Plan. The Bhadravati Steel Works is being converted to produce alloy, tool and special steel, and a separate plant for it at Durgapur is nearing completion. In regard to petroleum, the Barauni refinery has just been commissioned. Construction of the third public sector refinery at Koyali is progressing and it should be completed by the end of 1965. Cochin refinery is also expected to be completed by the end of 1965.

About petro-chemicals, large petro-chemical complexes have been planned so far, one in the public sector around Koyali refinery in Gujarat and the other in the private sector near Bombay.

In the matter of machinery making, the Tiruchi Boiler Factory will start production in 1965. The fifth unit of the Hindustan Machine Tools at Hyderabad will also go into production this year. The surgical Instruments Plant at Madras will be commissioned in the middle of 1965. There is the Heavy Structural Works in regard to which we have entered into an agreement with Austria. And then there is the Czech Foundry Forge at Wardha, which is also to be constructed. These are some of the examples which indicate what is being done and what we would achieve in the course of about a couple of years in regard to certain plants and in a longer period in regard to other plants. This is a sector in which we have naturally to depend more on the public sector.

The public sector has to expand considerably both as a matter of policy and also because it is not possible for outsiders to invest huge sums of money which are needed for setting up these basic industries. It is also in a way easier for the Government to enter into collaboration with other governments on government-to-government basis. And, therefore, we have to expand our public sector and these public sector projects will come to fruition to serve as the base of our industries and the industrial economy in the country. I would also like the private sector to grow, and naturally, they have to function in the background of our social objectives. It is also true that they will have to be given every opportunity to develop. And incentives may also have to be given so that they can increase their production.

Our fiscal policy is oriented towards greater production as also towards helping the weaker elements of our society. The various measures of proposals of our Budget indicate that for greater production incentives will be provided. The incentives are given mainly on the basis of production.

There may be—there may not have been—a large reduction or any special reduction in the corporate sector so far as taxes are concerned, but what is most important is increased production and for that, the Budget proposals do contain various incentives.

In regard to agriculture, there is no doubt that we had to face a difficult food situation a few months back. I do not say that everything is now all right. Things are still difficult. Yet, it must be said that we have turned the corner. There are foodgrains available in the market, and the prices also have not gone up recently. It is, of course, unfortunate that we have to continue to import and there seems to be no alternative for us for some time to come except to add to our indigenous production through imports and serve the needs of our people. It is essential especially in order to build up a buffer stock. It helps in getting over the lean periods and it also acts as a check and some kind of regulation on the trends of the market. Luckily, we have had very good rice crops, over 39 million tonnes, perhaps the highest production of rice, this year. We expect that we will have a good wheat crop also. And in the matter of rice, we have procured rice, and our target of procurement is about 19 lakh tonnes. We have so far procured about eight lakh tonnes but this procurement will continue and this will help us in building up a buffer stock. In regard to wheat, we have not yet taken a final decision but we will be building up stocks of foodgrains. Naturally, they will have to be procured from the surplus States. It is open to the deficit States also to make purchases, if they so like. We have our Food Corporation set-up which would also enter into the market. There is going to be no monopoly procurement by the Food corporation but it would also enter into the field along with others. I, therefore, hope, sir, that in this year (1965) we would have solved one of our most intricate problems and that there will be an easy situation so far as foodgrains are concerned. Of course, imports are there but in fact the Government of India does not want that we should have to import for a long time to come. We have naturally to increase our agricultural production and for that it is essential that the necessary inputs, the necessary ingredients for agricultural production should be provided to the farmer, whether it is fertiliser or water or good seeds or similar other things. These things are very important and it has to be seen that these things reach the farmers in time. And it is important for the administration, the district administration, to take a special interest in it. There should be better coordination between the departments concerned, particularly those which deal with the panchayats.

Our target of foodgrains production for the Third Five Year Plan was 92 million tonnes. I am sorry to say that last year it has only been 80 million tonnes.

This indicates that we have to go very far. In fact, the Memorandum of the Fourth Five Year Plan has fixed the target at 120 million tonnes. Well, I do not think that it is impossible to achieve it.

Yet great efforts will have to be made and everyone of us will have to cooperate in the matter. I say "us" because Members of Parliament can help in this matter a great deal. They are the representatives of the people and they have to create an atmosphere in which the farmer, the peasant, will be interested in increasing agricultural production. It is essential that we generate a feeling in him that it is good for him to produce more and it is in the best interests of the country to have greater agricultural production. Sometimes it is not the physical need but perhaps a mental resolve, a mental resolution that he will do his utmost to increase the production in the larger interest of the country which would work as a magic. We have to create the mental resolution amongst our farmers. I have no doubt that if we increase our production, it would lead to stability in prices and it would also help in creating general prosperity all round, and then naturally it would mean less of dependence on foreign countries.

Sir, in regard to external affairs, we have always tried that the Geneva Agreement on Indochina should be adhered to; that there should be no breach of the Agreement and that there should be no conflict. Unfortunately, recently a new development has already arisen and the position seems to be fairly delicate. In that context we had appealed and expressed our views that two things are absolutely essential to resolve this problem : First, the hostilities which are going on at present should come to an end and the two parties should stop fighting. Secondly, there should be a Geneva-type conference. We feel that those who are not directly interested might also meet so that there is a dialogue, there is a talk, there is a discussion and there might be mutual consultations and talks also which would lead us to finding some kind of solution. We have also written to different Governments, different countries in this regard, and I might say that there is a generally favourable response from those countries. They have generally supported the idea that there should be some kind of joint appeal in order to end the present hostilities, and they also feel that there should be some kind of a conference. I think it is in the interest of world peace that these suggestions are accepted, and we will do our level best to move in this matter and see that something positive is done.

Our policy of non-alignment and peaceful co-existence is strongly and fully endorsed and is going to continue as our basic policy. As a non-aligned country we should have the authority to think independently. Secondly, non-alignment helps us in expanding the sphere of peace. It is essential that if we want to have peace it would be better for as large a number of countries as possible to keep out of the power blocs. And we, therefore, feel that our policy of non-alignment is necessary, useful and good for the country. Peaceful co-existence means that we do believe that it is not possible to have one kind of pattern throughout the world. It is not possible to regiment the thinking of man. The human being has got this special faculty of thinking and, therefore, there will be different patterns, different systems of administration and different forms of government. It is therefore, important that in spite of the different ways of thinking, different approaches, different ideologies, the world should live in peace and different countries should live as good neighbours.

The United Nations, in spite of its failings, has been a hope for the world. It has done many useful things and averted a number of critical moments when the world might have plunged into war. But recently, in regard to article 19, a new difficulty, a new complication has arisen. I do not want to go into that particular matter in detail because the House is aware of the developments. Recently they have formed a Committee to go into this matter. India is also a member of this Committee. We will try to contribute our mite.

We have had a number of distinguished guests from abroad during the last five or six months in our country. I am glad to say that our relations with our neighbouring countries have considerably improved. There may be some differences still remaining but by and large our relations are better and it is essential that we should have the best of relations with our neighbouring countries—Ceylon, Nepal, Burma, Afghanistan. The dignitaries, the Heads of these States, the Prime Ministers of these countries, have visited India. We have met them, have had talks and discussions with them and I must say that these talks have been very useful and we have definitely come closer to each other. I might also say that I have received invitations from a number of countries. It is not possible for me to visit all the countries from where I have received invitations but I have decided to visit the Soviet Republic and I have also received an invitation from the President of the United States and I would also be going there.

In regard to the language question, I would say that it is a very delicate issue. It has aroused feelings throughout the country, especially in the southern parts of India. People are naturally deeply attached to their mother-tongue and there is absolutely no question of displacing or replacing the mother-tongue spoken in different States. When I referred to misapprehension, I said it especially in regard to the use of the State language, or the mother-tongue, because some Tamil papers and some other pamphlets, etc., wrote that Tamil goes and Hindi comes, that Hindi will replace Tamil. There were even slogans to this effect shouted by some people in Madras. So this was a clear case of misapprehension. In so far as the State language is concerned, it is there, it has to be there and the Government of India will naturally like to give all possible encouragement to the development of the State languages. It is essential and we have certainly no objection to it. Almost all the State Governments have accepted or adopted the policy of introducing the State language as the official language of the State, and I know that in course of time all the State languages will become the principal languages for official purposes. As to the medium of instruction, of course, it is left to the State Governments. So therefore, in so far as the State languages are concerned, there can be no doubt at all in the mind of anyone that there is any question of replacing those languages by Hindi.

The second point is about the use of English. On January 26, 1965, it was, of course, officially announced, in terms of the provisions of the constitution, Hindi would be the official language of the Union and, if the Hon'ble members will see, there was no other action taken which could create any kind of confusion. I am told about some circulars in Hindi. Well, even if some circulars were issued, it should not have resulted in such violent action. Our mistakes could have been pointed out. I remember, when I was in charge of the Communications Ministry, a money order form was brought to my knowledge ; it was printed in Hindi only. Immediately I got it rectified and money order forms in Hindi were completely stopped from being sent to the south; forms in English were introduced there. So, even if there were certain discrepancies, or some mistakes made, it should have been pointed out to us, and we would have immediately rectified it. So there has been some cause for misapprehension, and as Mr. Annadurai rightly said, there has been a genuine apprehension also of the imposition of Hindi. I have made it categorically clear that we will abide by the wishes of and the assurances given by the late Prime Minister, Pandit Jawaharlal Nehru. I stand by it and we will certainly consider as to how to do it, how to implement it. That is one point which is under our consideration. Along with that, of course, we will have to realise that this country should have a link language. I am glad that Mr. Annadurai has said that he is not against Hindi as such, but he wants that it should not be spread through the help of the Government. Well, I would not like to say anything about that, but I do wish and hope that after some time he might like to reconsider his view even in regard to this particular matter. I do agree that there should be non-official effort, as big an effort as possible., for the teaching and propagation of Hindi. All the same it is important that English has to continue, it will continue. In terms of the Official Languages Act, English is to continue as an associate language, and there will be no difficulty at all for anyone who does not know Hindi, whether he is functioning here in the Secretariat, or in any other all-India office in any other part of the country. There will be no handicap at all in the matter of recruitment. There will be no handicap at all in the matter of promotion etc., because the officer does not know Hindi. I mean, these assurances are there. And then, between one State and the other English could be used, and is to be used, but in regard to the Center it is again open to the State Governments to use English. Between one State and another, if they agree to correspond with each other in a particular language, they are free to do so. For example, between Rajasthan and Uttar Pradesh, if they want to correspond with each other in Hindi, they might do so. But so far as the Centre is concerned, it has to be both in English as well as in Hindi.

With these assurances, Sir, I do not think there should be any kind of fear or apprehension in the minds of the people of Madras. I would like to say that we are considering several matters in this connection. The question of the three-language formula is there; then some other matters, for example, the medium of examination in different languages. Well, we will examine all these matters; we will study them and then come to definite conclusions. The issue of language is such that it is better to take a cool and calculated view of things, and we must consider its various aspects and implications. I do hope that the students of Madras will now at least see things in the correct perspective. They have by and large withdrawn their strike, and I have extended my congratulations to them. Still there is some trouble somewhere; it may not be especially due to the language problem as such; it perhaps might be because of the cases of the detentions, etc. I would appeal to them that they must wait and see. They should not take any hurried action. I have no doubt that the Madras Government will consider all their suggestions more sympathetically. It would be in the best interests of the students as well as the State and the country that they do not resort to any kind of direct action.

I am glad that Shri Annadurai said that he did not want to interfere with the students or that he did not want to encourage them. It is indeed, from my point of view, very good and very satisfactory. I also do not believe that students as such should take direct part in politics. For youth outside the colleges and schools it is different. But so long as students are studying in universities and colleges and schools, they should not take an active part or associate themselves with any political organisation. They may study peacefully and quietly, and after they have completed their studies, they will be free to associate themselves with any political party or political organisation. I would humbly appeal that language should serve as a cementing force. Language is to unite; it is not to disunite. Language has to integrate and not to disintegrate, and, therefore, we have to keep the question of unity first and foremost in our minds. I would without taking much time of this House, Sir, appeal to Members of Parliament that they should always have the vision of a united India. In their mind's eye, they should carry an image of the whole country a map which has no internal dividing lines but only the frontiers of this vast and varied and yet united land.

INDIRA GANDHI

SMT. INDIRA GANDHI was born on 19th November, 1917 at Allahabad to Pandit Jawahar Lal Nehru and Kamla Nehra. She was the 4th prime minister of India and was also the first and, to date, only female prime minister of India. The Nehru family can trace their ancestry to the Brahmins of Jammu and Kashmir and Delhi. Indira's grandfather Motilal Nehru was a wealthy barrister of Allahabad in Uttar Pradesh.

She was their only child. Nehru was one of the most prominent members of the Indian National Congress in pre-Gandhi times and would go on to author the Nehru Report, the people's choice for a future Indian system of government as opposed to the British system. Her father Jawaharlal Nehru was a well-educated lawyer and was a popular leader of the Indian Independence Movement. At the time of Indira's birth, Nehru entered the independence movement under the leadership of Mahatma Gandhi. Nehru's long tenure in office gave continuity and cohesion to India's domestic and foreign policies, but as his health deteriorated, concerns over who might inherit his mantle or what might befall India after he left office frequently surfaced in political circles.

In 1936, her mother, Kamala Nehru, finally succumbed to tuberculosis after a long struggle. Indira was 18 at the time and thus never experienced a stable family life during her childhood. She attended prominent Indian, European and British schools like Santiniketan, Badminton School and Oxford, but she showed no incandescence for academics, and was detained from obtaining a degree. While studying at Somerville College, University of Oxford, England, during the late 1930s, she became a member of the radical pro-independence London based India League. In her years in continental Europe and the UK, she met Feroze Gandhi,a Congress activist. Nehru was not happy; Kamala was dead already or dying. Just before the beginning of the Quit India Movement - the final, all-out national revolt launched by Mahatma Gandhi and the Congress Party.

In September 1942 they were arrested by the British authorities and detained without charge. She was ultimately released on 13 May 1943 having spent over 243 days in jail. In 1944, she gave birth to Rajiv Gandhi with Feroze Gandhi, and followed by Sanjay Gandhi.

During the chaotic Partition of India in 1947, she helped organize refugee camps and provide medical care for the millions of refugees from Pakistan. This was her first exercise in major public service, and a valuable experience for the tumult of the coming years. The couple later settled in Allahabad where Feroze worked for a Congress Party newspaper and an insurance company. Their marriage started out well, but deteriorated later as Gandhi moved to New Delhi to be at the side of her father, now the Prime Minister, who was living alone in a high-pressure environment at Teen Murti Bhavan. She became his confidante, secretary and nurse. Her sons lived with her, but she eventually became permanently separated from Feroze, though they remained married.

When India's first general election approached in 1951, Gandhi managed the campaigns of both Nehru and her husband, who was contesting the constituency of Rae Bareilly. Feroze had not consulted Nehru on his choice to run, and even though he was elected, he opted to live in a separate house in Delhi. Feroze quickly developed a reputation for being a fighter against corruption by exposing a major scandal in the nationalized insurance industry, resulting in the resignation of the Finance Minister, a Nehru aide.

At the height of the tension, Gandhi and her husband separated. However, in 1958, shortly after re-election, Feroze suffered a heart attack, which dramatically healed their broken marriage. At his side to help him recuperate in Kashmir, their family grew closer. But Feroze died on September 8, 1960, while Gandhi was abroad with Nehru on a foreign visit.

During 1959 and 1960, Gandhi ran for and was elected the President of the Indian National Congress. Her term of office was uneventful. She also acted as her father's chief of staff. Nehru was known as a vocal opponent of nepotism, and she did not contest a seat in the 1962 elections.

After his death, the Congress Caucus, also known as the Syndicate, chose Lal Bahadur Shastri as prime minister in June 1964. A mild-mannered person, Shastri adhered to Gandhian principles of simplicity of life and dedication to the service of the country. His short period of leadership was beset with three major crises: widespread food shortages, violent anti-Hindi demonstrations in the state of Madras (as Tamil Nadu was then called) that were quelled by the army, and the second war with Pakistan over Kashmir. Shastri's premiership was cut short when he died of a heart attack on January 11, 1966, the day after having signed the Soviet-brokered Tashkent Declaration. The agreement required both sides to withdraw all armed personnel by February 26, 1966, to the positions they had held prior to August 5, 1965, and to observe the cease-fire line.

Indira Gandhi held a cabinet portfolio as minister of information and broadcasting in Shastri's government. She was the only child of Nehru, who was also her mentor in the nationalist movement. The Syndicate selected her as prime minister when Shastri died in 1966 even though her eligibility was challenged by Morarji Desai, a veteran nationalist and long-time aspirant to that office. The Congress "bosses" were apparently looking for a leading figure acceptable to the masses, who could command general support during the next general election but who would also acquiesce to their guidance. Hardly had Indira Gandhi begun in office than she encountered a series of problems that defied easy solutions: Mizo tribal uprisings in the northeast; famine, labor unrest, and misery among the poor in the wake of rupee devaluation; and agitation in Punjab for linguistic and religious separatism.

In the fourth general election in February 1967, the Congress majority was greatly reduced when it secured only 54 percent of the parliamentary seats, and non-Congress ministries were established in Bihar, Kerala, Orissa, Madras, Punjab, and West Bengal the next month. A Congress-led coalition government collapsed in Uttar Pradesh, while in April Rajasthan was brought under President's Rule—direct central government rule. Seeking to eradicate poverty, Mrs. Gandhi pursued a vigorous policy in 1969 of land reform and placed a ceiling on personal income, private property, and corporate profits. She also nationalized the major banks, a bold step amidst a growing rift between herself and the party elders. The Congress expelled her for "indiscipline" on November 12, 1969, an action that split the party into two factions: the Congress (O)—for Organisation—under Desai, and the Congress (R)—for Requisition—under Gandhi. She continued as prime minister with support from communists, Sikhs, and regional parties.

Indira Gandhi campaigned fiercely on the platform "eliminate poverty" (*garibi hatao*) during the fifth general election in March 1971, and the Congress (R) gained a large majority in Parliament against her former party leaders whose slogan was "eliminate Indira" (*Indira hatao*). India's decisive victory over Pakistan in the third war over Kashmir in December 1971, and Gandhi's insistence that the 10 million refugees from Bangladesh be sent back to their country generated a national surge in her popularity, later confirmed by her party's gains in state elections in 1972. She had firmly established herself at the pinnacle of power, overcoming challenges from the Congress (O), the Supreme Court, and the state chief ministers in the early 1970s. The more solidified her monopoly of power became, the more egregious was her intolerance of criticisms, even when they were deserved. As head of her party and the government, Gandhi nominated and removed the chief ministers at will and frequently reshuffled the portfolios of her own cabinet members. Ignoring their obligations to their constituencies, party members competed with each other in parading their loyalty to Gandhi, whose personal approval alone seemed crucial to their survival. In August 1971, Gandhi signed the twenty-year Treaty of Peace, Friendship, and Cooperation with the Soviet Union because ties with the United States, which had improved in Nehru's later years, had eroded.

Neither Gandhi's consolidation of power, nor her imperious style of administration, nor even her rhetoric of radical reforms was enough to meet the deepening economic crisis spawned by the enormous cost of the 1971 war. A huge additional outlay was needed to manage the refugees, the crop failures in 1972 and 1973, the skyrocketing world oil prices in 1973-74, and the overall drop in industrial output despite a surplus of scientifically and technically trained personnel. No immediate sign of economic recovery or equity was visible despite a loan obtained from the International Monetary Fund in 1974. Both Gandhi's office and character came under severe tests, beginning with railroad employee strikes, national civil disobedience advocated by J.P. Narayan, defeat of her party in Gujarat by a coalition of parties calling itself the Janata Morcha (People's Front), an all-party, no-confidence motion in Parliament, and, finally, a writ issued by the Allahabad High Court invalidating her 1971 election and making her ineligible to occupy her seat for six years.

What had once seemed a remote possibility took place on June 25, 1975: the president declared an Emergency and the government suspended civil rights. Because the nation's president, Fakhruddin Ali Ahmed (1974-77), and Gandhi's own party members in Parliament were amenable to her personal influence, Gandhi had little trouble in pushing through amendments to the constitution that exonerated her from any culpability, declaring President's Rule in Gujarat and Tamil Nadu where anti-Indira parties ruled, and jailing thousands of her opponents. In her need to trust and confide in someone during this extremely trying period, she turned to her younger son, Sanjay, who became an enthusiastic advocate of the Emergency. Under his watchful eyes, forced sterilization as a means of birth control was imposed on the poor, increased numbers of urban squatters and slum dwellers in Delhi were evicted in the name of beautification projects, and disgruntled workers were either disciplined or their wages frozen. The Reign of Terror, as some called it, continued until January 18, 1977, when Gandhi suddenly relaxed the Emergency, announced the next general election in March, and released her opponents from prison.

With elections only two months away, both J.P. Narayan and Morarji Desai reactivated the multiparty front, which campaigned as the Janata Party and rode anti-Emergency sentiment to secure a clear majority in the Lok Sabha (House of the People), the lower house of Parliament. Desai, a conservative Brahman, became India's fourth prime minister (1977-79), but his government, from its inception, became notorious for its factionalism and furious internal competition. As it promised, the Janata government restored freedom and democracy, but its inability to effect sound reforms or ameliorate poverty left people disillusioned. Desai lost the support of Janata's left-wing parties by the early summer of

1979, and several secular and liberal politicians abandoned him altogether, leaving him without a parliamentary majority. A no-confidence motion was about to be introduced in Parliament in July 1979, but he resigned his office; Desai's government was replaced by a coalition led by Chaudhury Charan Singh (prime minister in 1979-80). Although Singh's life-long ambition had been to become prime minister, his age and inefficiency were used against him, and his attempts at governing India proved futile; new elections were announced in January 1980.

Gandhi and her party, renamed Congress (I)—I for Indira—campaigned on the slogan "Elect a Government That Works!" and regained power. Sanjay Gandhi was elected to the Lok Sabha. Unlike during the Emergency, when India registered significant economic and industrial progress, Gandhi's return to power was hindered by a series of woes and tragedies, beginning with Sanjay's death in June 1980 while attempting to perform stunts in his private airplane. Secessionist forces in Punjab and in the northeast and the Soviet occupation of Afghanistan in December 1979 consumed her energy. She began to involve the armed forces in resolving violent domestic conflicts between 1980 and 1984. Indira Gandhi was awarded the Lenin Peace Prize (for 1983-84).

In May 1984, Sikh extremists occupied the Golden Temple in Amritsar, converting it into a haven for terrorists. Gandhi responded in early June when she launched Operation Bluestar, which killed and wounded hundreds of soldiers, insurgents, and civilians. Guarding against further challenges to her power, she removed the chief ministers of Jammu and Kashmir and Andhra Pradesh just months before her assassination by her Sikh bodyguards on October 31, 1984. The news of Indira Gandhi's assassination plunged New

Delhi and other parts of India into anti-Sikh riots for three days; several thousand Sikhs were killed.

WHAT EDUCATED WOMEN CAN DO AT THE GOLDEN JUBILEE CELEBRATIONS OF THE INDRAPRASTHA COLLEGE FOR WOMEN NEW DELHI, INDIA, NOVEMBER 23, 1974

AN ancient Sanskrit saying says, woman is the home and the home is the basis of society. It is as we build our homes that we can build our country. If the home is inadequate — either inadequate in material goods and necessities or inadequate in the sort of friendly, loving atmosphere that every child needs to grow and develop — then that country cannot have harm ony and no country which does not have harmony can grow in any direction at all.

That is why women's education is almost more important than the education of boys and men. We — and by "we" I do not mean only we in India but all the world — have neglected women education. It is fairly rece nt. Of course, not to you but when I was a child, the story of early days of women's education in England, for instance, was very current.

Everybody remembered what had happened in the early days.

I remember what used to happen here. I still remember the days when living in old Delhi even as a small child of seven or eight. I had to go ou t in a doli if I left the house. We just did not walk. Girls did not walk in the streets. First, you had your sari with which you covered your head, then you had another shawl or something with which you covered your hand and all the body, then you had a white shawl, with which every thing was covered again although your face was open fortunately. Then you were i n the doli, which again was covered by another cloth. And this was in a family or community which did not observe purdah of any kind at all. In fact, all our social functions always were mixed functions but this was the atmosphere of the city and of the country.

Now, we have got education and there is a debate all over the country whether this education is adequate to the needs of society or the needs of our young people. I am one of those who always believe that education needs a thorough overhauling. But at the same time, I think that everything in our education is not bad, that even the present education has produced very fine men and women, specially scientists and experts in different fields, who are in great demand all over the world and even in the most affluent countries. Many of our young people leave us and go abroad because they get higher salaries, they get better conditions of work.

But it is not all a one-sided business because there

are many who are persuaded and cajoled to go even when they are reluctant. We know of first class students, especially in medicine or nuclear energy for instance, they are approached long before they have passed out and offered all kinds of inducements to go out. Now, that shows that people do consider that they have a standard of knowledge and capability which will be useful any where in the world.

So, that is why I say that there is something worthwhile. It also shows that our own ancient philosophy has taught us that nothing in life is entirely bad or entirely good. Everything is somewhat of a mixture and it depends on us and our capability how we can extract the good, how we can make use of what is around us. There are people who through observation can learn from anything that is around them. There are others who can be surrounded by the most fascinating people, the most wonderful books, and other things and who yet remain quite closed in and they are unable to take anything from this wealth around them.

Our country is a very rich country. It is rich in culture, it is rich in many old traditions — old and even modern tradition. Of course, it has a lot of bad things too and some of the bad things are in the society — superstition, which has grown over the years and which sometimes clouds over the shining brightness of ancient thought and values, eternal values. Then, of course, there is the physical poverty of large numbers of our people. That is something which is ugly and that hampers the growth of millions of young boys and girls. Now, all these bad things we have to fight against and that is what we are doing since Independence.

But, we must not allow this dark side of the picture which, by the way, exists in every country in the world. Even the most rich country in the world has its dark side, but usually other people hide their dark sides and they try to project the shining side or the side of achievement. Here in India, we seem to want to project the worst side of society. Before anybody does anything, he has to have, of course, knowledge and capability, but along with it he has to have a certain amount of pride in what he or she is doing. He has to have self-confidence in his own ability. If your teacher tells, "You cannot do this," even if you are a very bright student I think every time you will find, it will be more and more difficult for you to do it. But if your teacher encourages saying, "Go along you have done very good work, now try a little harder," then you will try a little harder and you will be able to do it. And it is the same with societies and with countries.

This country, India, has had remarkable achievements to its credit, of course in ancient times, but even in modern times, I think there are a few modern stories, success stories, which are as fascinating as the success story of our country. It is true that we have not banished poverty, we have not banished many of our social ills, but if you compare us to what we were just about 27 years ago, I think that you will not find a single other country that has been able to achieve so much under the most difficult circumstances.

Today, we are passing through specially dark days. But these are not dark days for India alone. Except for the countries which call themselves socialist and about which we do not really know very much, every other country has the same sort of economic problems, which we have. Only a few countries, which have very small populations, have no unemployment. Otherwise, the rich countries also today have unemployment. They have shortages of essential articles. They have shortages even of food.

I do not know how many of you know that the countries of Western Europe and Japan import 41 per cent of their food needs, whereas India imports just under two per cent. Yet, somehow we ourselves project an image that India is out with the begging bowl. And naturally when we ourselves say it, other people will say it much louder and much stronger. It is true, of course, that our two per cent is pretty big because we are a very big country and we have a far bigger population than almost any country in the world with the exception of China. We have to see and you, the educated women, because it is great privilege for you to have higher education, you have to try and see our problems in the perspective of what has happened here in this country and what is happening all over the world.

There is today great admiration for certain things that have happened in other countries where the society is quite differently formed, where no dissent is allowed. The same people who admire that system or the achievements of that system are the ones who say there is dictatorship here even though, I think, nobody has yet been able to point out to me which country has more freedom of expression or action. So, something is said and a lot of people without thinking keep on repeating it with additions until an entirely distorted picture of the country and of our people is presented.

As I said, we do have many shortcomings, whether it is the government, whether it is the society. Some are due to our traditions because, as I said, not all tradition is good. And one of the biggest responsibilities of the educated women today is how to synthesise what has been valuable and timeless in our ancient traditions with what is good and valuable in modern thought. All that is modern is not good just as all that is old is neither all good nor all bad. We have to decide, not once and for all but almost every week, every month what is coming out that is good and useful to our country and what of the old we can keep and enshrine in our society. To be modern, most people think that it is something of a manner of dress or a manner of speaking or certain habits and customs, but that is not really being modern. It is a very superficial part of modernity.

For instance, when I cut my hair, it was because of the sort of life that I was leading. We were all in the movement. You simply could not have long hair and go in the villages and wash it every day. So, when you lead a life, a particular kind of life, your clothes, your everything has to fit into that life if you are to be efficient. If you have to go in the villages and you have to bother whether your clothes are going to be dirty, then you cannot be a good worker. You have to forget everything of that kind. That is why, gradually, clothes and so on have changed in some countries because of the changes in the life-style. Does it suit our life-style or what we want to do or not? If it does, maybe we have to adopt some of these things not merely because it is done in another country and perhaps for another purpose. But what clothes we wear is really quite unimportant. What is important is how we are thinking.

Sometimes, I am very sad that even people who do science are quite unscientific in their thinking and in their other actions — not what they are doing in the laboratories but how they live at home or their attitudes towards other people. Now, for India to become what we want it to become with a modern, rational society and firmly based on what is good in our ancient tradition and in our soil, for this we have to have a thinking public, thinking young women who are not content to accept what comes from any part of the world but are willing to listen to it, to analyse it and to decide whether it is to be accepted or whether it is to be thrown out and this is the sort of education which we want, which enables our young people to adjust to this changing world and to be able to contribute to it.

Some people think that only by taking up very high jobs, you are doing something important or you are doing national service. But we all know that the most complex machinery will be ineffective if one small screw is not working as it should and that screw is just as important as any big part. It is the same in national life. There is no job that is too small; there is no person who is too small. Everybody has something to do. And if he or she does it well, then the country will run well.

In our superstition, we have thought that some work is dirty work. For instance, sweeping has been regarded as dirty. Only some people can do it; others should not do it. Now we find that manure is the most valuable thing that the world has today and many of the world's economies are shaking because there is not enough fertilizer — and not just the chemical fertilizer but the ordinary manure, night-soil and all that sort of thing, things which were considered dirty.

Now it shows how beautifully balanced the world was with everything fitted in with something else. Everything, whether dirty or small, had a purpose. We, with our science and technology, have tried to — not purposely, but somehow, we have created an imbalance and that is what is troubling, on a big scale, the economies of the world and also people and individuals. They are feeling alienated from their societies, not only in India but almost in every country in the world, except in places where the whole purpose of education and government has to be to make the people conform to just one idea. We are told that people there are very happy in whatever they are doing. If they are told to clean the streets, well, if he is a professor he has to clean the streets, if he is a scientist he has to do it, and we were told that they are happy doing it. Well, if they are happy, it is alright.

But I do not think in India we can have that kind of society where people are forced to do things because we think that they can be forced maybe for 25 years, maybe for 50 years, but sometime or the other there will be an explosion. In our society, we allow lots of smaller explosions because we think that that will guard the basic stability and progress of society and prevent it from having the kind of chaotic explosion which can retard our progress and harmony in the country.

So, I hope that all of you who have this great advantage of education will not only do whatever work you are doing keeping the national interests in view, but you will make your own contribution to creating peace and harmony, to bringing beauty in the lives of our people and our country. I think this is the special responsibility of the women of India. We want to do a great deal for our country, but we have never regarded India as isolated from the rest of the world. What we want to do is to make a better world. So, we have to see India's problems in the perspective of the larger world problems.

It has given me great pleasure to be with you here. I give my warm congratulations to those who are doing well and my very good wishes to all the others that they will also do much better. This college has had a high reputation but we must always see that we do better than those who were there before us. So, good luck and good wishes to you.

TRUE LIBERATION OF WOMEN AT THE INAUGURATION OF THE ALLINDIA WOMEN'S CONFERENCE BUILDING COMPLEX NEW DELHI, INDIA, MARCH 26, 1980

FOR several decades the All-India Women's Conference has been the organized voice of the women of India. I have never been a member of any women's organization but have been interested enough to keep track of their activities and to lend the helping hand whenever I could.

I am glad that at long last the All-India Women's Conference has a home of its own and it is named after one of the best known and most remarkable women of our times, Sarojini Naidu, feminine to the core but well able to hold her own in the world of men, whether in letters or in politics.

To add to the importance of the occasion and to give it a touch of elegance, we have in our midst His Highness the Aga Khan and Her Highness the Begum Aga Khan. They are friends of India and have founded or encouraged many projects for education, health and other aspects of welfare. But for their timely and generous help, this complex would not have been ready today. Nor would we have before us the attractive Aga Khan Hall. We welcome them and wish them well in their work.

I see before me a number of eminent women who have distinguished themselves in various professions — in social work, in education, in science, in administration, in law and, of course, in politics. They must all feel gratified to see the completion of this building. I have often said that I am not a feminist. Yet, in my concern for the underprivileged, how can I ignore women who, since the beginning of history, have been dominated over and discriminated against in social customs and in laws. How insidious and all-pervasive is this attitude of male' superiority is revealed in the vocabulary of the languages the world over. And this is unquestioningly accepted and acquiesced in by all but a minuscule minority of men and also women. Currently I am reading a book titled *World and Women*. I learned from it what Mr. Ling White, the President of Mills College in the USA, wrote of the use of masculine generic pronouns. I quote: "The penetration of the habit of language into the minds of little girls as they grow up to be women is more profound than most people, including most women, have realized. For, it implies that personality is really a male attribute and that women are a sub or a human sub-species." The author goes on to say that it is time we looked more carefully where the thoughtless use of stereotypes is taking us. "Man as leader, woman as follower; man as producer, woman as consumer; man as strength, woman as weakness; this is the cosmography that has brought us to man as aggressor and humanity the victim."

Hence, by excluding women, men are depriving themselves of a fuller emancipation or growth for themselves.

In the West, women's so-called freedom is often equated with imitation of man. Frankly, I feel that is merely an exchange of one kind of bondage for another. To be liberated, woman must feel free to be herself, not in rivalry to man but in the context of her own capacity and her personality. We need women to be more interested, more alive and more active not because they are women but because they do comprise half the human race. Whether they like it or not, they cannot escape their responsibility nor should they be denied its benefits. Indian women are traditionally conservative but they also have the genius of synthesis, to adapt and to absorb. That is what gives them resilience to face suffering and to meet upheavals with a degree of calm, to change constantly and yet remain changeless, which is the quality of India herself.

Today's major concerns are: first, economic and social inequality and injustice between the affluent and developing countries and within countries. Secondly, the anxiety whether human wisdom will prevail over what can only be called a death wish in which the desire to dominate expresses itself in countless ways, the most dangerous being the armament race. And, thirdly, the need to protect this, our only Earth, from human rapacity and exploitation. Only recently have we awakened to the awareness of ancient truths regarding our own utter dependence on the balance of Nature and its resources.

These enormous challenges cannot be met only by some sections, however advanced they may be, while others pull in different directions or watch apathetically. The effort has to be a universal one, conscious and concerted, considering no one too small to contribute. The effort must embrace all nationalities and all classes regardless of religion, caste or sex.

There is no time to lose and it involves a tremendous task of educating. We want to walk together and in step with all others, but if men hesitate, should not women show the way? So, while complimenting the All-India Women's Conference, especially its President, Smt. Lakshmi Raghuramaiah, on their achievements, I dedicate to the nation this building complex of the All-India Women's Conference.

AT THE SEVENTH CONFERENCE OF HEADS OF STATE OR GOVERNMENT OF NON-ALIGNED COUNTRIES, NEW DELHI, MARCH 7, 1983

WHEN assuming the reins of government in 1946, my father, Jawaharlal Nehru, declared India's determination "to keep away from the power blocs or groups, aligned against one another, which have led in the past to world wars and which may again lead to disasters on an even vaster scale." Later, he explained that once "foreign relations go out of your hands into the charge of somebody else, to that extent and in that measure you are not independent... So our policy will continue to be not only to keep away from alignments, but also to try to make friendly co-operation possible. We approach the whole world on a friendly basis."

As more countries became free, the number of those who believed in peaceful coexistence and wished to keep out of military alliances increased steadily. It was natural for these nonaligned countries to come together, not to form another bloc but to raise the voices of the exploited millions through a moral and political movement.

The very growth in the membership of our Movement -twenty-five in Belgrade, a hundred now - proves that nonalignment meets a felt need of vast numbers of people In various continents.

Its significance is not to be measured by the number of divisions or the megatons of destructive power we command but by the intensity with which we desire peace and freedom, development and international justice.

Other governments may have conflicting opinions on right and wrong. We, the nonaligned have chosen peace, which surely is the right and inevitable choice. We have sought and continue to seek friendship with all, except governments which are racist or threaten the hard-earned freedom of others. Nonalignment is not vague, not negative, not neutral. Nonalignment is national Independence and freedom. It stands for peace and the avoidance of confrontation. It aims at keeping away from military alliances. it means equality among nations and the democratization of international relations, economic and political. It wants global co-operation for development on the basis of mutual benefit. It is a strategy for the recognition and preservation of the world's diversity.

... Humankind is balancing on the brink of the collapse of the world economic system and annihilation through nuclear war. Should these tragedies occur, can anyone of us, large, small. rich or poor, from North or South, West or East, hope to escape? Let us analyze the economic crisis. We of the developing world have no margin of safety. We shall be the first and worst sufferers in any economic background. In this interdependent world, where you cannot "stir a flower without troubling a star," even the most affluent are not immune to such disturbances.

... Development, independence, disarmament and peace are closely related. Can there be peace alongside nuclear weapons? Without peace, my father said, all our dreams of development turn to ashes. It has been pointed out that global military expenditure is 20 times the total official development assistance. Each day, each hour, the size and the lethality of nuclear weapons increase. A nuclear aircraft carrier costs $ 4 billion, which is more than the GNP of 53 countries. The hood of the cobra is spread. Humankind watches in frozen fear, hoping against hope that it will not strike. Never before has the earth faced so much death and danger.

The destructive power contained in nuclear stockpiles can kill human life, indeed all life, many times over and might well prevent its reappearance for ages to come. Terrifying is the vividness of such descriptions by scientists. Yet, some statesmen and strategists art as though there is not much difference between these and the earlier artillery pieces. The arms race continues because of the pursuit of power and desire for one upmanship, and also because many industries and interests flourish on it. More recently, the notion has been propagated that tactial nuclear weapons are usable in "limited wars." Powerful States propagate the untenable doctrine of deterrence. New areas are being brought into the scope of strategic groupings, military blocs and alliances. New bases and facilities are being established. That is why our responses must be surer, swifter and sharper.

The desire for peace is universal even within countries which themselves produce nuclear weapons and in those where they are deployed. The Nonaligned Movement is history's biggest peace movement. It welcomes these spontaneous upsurges of peoples. But Governments persist in propounding, practicing and pursuing the self-same strategic interests, spheres of influence, balance of power, and tutelary relations reminiscent of the earlier theory of divine right.

The paradox of our age is that while weapons become increasingly sophisticated, minds remain imprisoned in ideas of simpler times. Technically, the colonial age has ended. But the wish to dominate persists. Neo-colonialism comes wrapped in all types of packages-in technology and communications, commerce and culture. It takes boldness and integrity to resist it. There are intense political and economic pressures. The limited economic viability, indeed the very survival of many of the nonaligned, especially those with small populations, is threatened through artificial barriers In trade, technology transfer and access to resources. It should be within our ability to devise measures to help these small nations to maintain their independence and nonalignment.

Only with coexistence can there be any existence. We regard non-interference and non-intervention as basic laws of international behavior. Yet different types of interventions, open or covert, do take place in Asia, in Africa, in Latin America. They are all intolerable and unacceptable. Interference leads to intervention and one intervention often attracts another. No single power or group of powers has the justification or moral authority to so interfere or intervene. You cannot condemn one instance but condone another. Each situation has its own origins. Whatever they be, solutions must be political and peaceful. All States must abide by the principle that force or the threat of force will not be used against the territorial integrity or political independence of another state.

... Our plans for a better life for each of our peoples depend on world peace and the reversal of the arms race. Negotiations confined to a closed circle of nuclear-weapon powers have made little progress. We are non-nuclear States, who want nuclear energy used only for peace. But we too have a right to live and be heard. In the name of humanity and on behalf of us all, I call upon nuclear -weapon powers to give up the use of nuclear weapons in any circumstances; suspend all nuclear weapons: and resume disarmament negotiations with determination to reach agreement.

...Nationalism does not detach us from our common humanity. What a marvelous opportunity is ours with the immense knowledge and Increasing capability. Let us grasp it, though it be in the midst of dangers. Faith in the future has brought so many across the continents and the oceans to meet here. We are here because we do believe that minds and attitudes can and must be changed and the injustice and suffering can and must be diminished. Our world is small but it has room for all of us to live together and to improve the quality of the lives for our peoples in peace and beauty.

MORARJI DESAI

SHRI MORARJI DESAI was born into an Anavil Brahmin family in Bhadeli, Valsad in Bombay Presidency (now in Gujarat). After graduating from Wilson College, Bombay, he joined the civil service in Gujarat. Later, he left the service of the British in 1924 and joined the civil disobedience movement against British rule in India in 1930. He spent many years in jail during the freedom struggle and owing to his sharp leadership skills and tough spirit, he became a favourite amongst freedom-fighters and an important leader of the Indian National Congress in Gujarat. When provincial elections were held in 1934 and 1937, Desai was elected and served as the Revenue Minister and Home Minister of the then Bombay Presidency.

Before the independence of India, he became Bombay's Home Minister and later was elected as Chief Minister of Bombay in 1952. The state was home to Marathi linguistic movements, with calls for the creation of a separate linguistic state. Considered as a tough leader, Desai was also known for pioneering beliefs and enforcing strict discipline and authority and thus possessed a radical mindset. By Desai's orders in 1960, a violent demonstration by the Samyukta Maharashtra Samiti was fired upon by the police resulting in the deaths of 105 demonstrators. Many rioters were killed in the incident leading to public outrage that shook the central government. The incident led to the formation of the present State of Maharashtra.

As Home Minister, Desai outlawed any portrayals of indecency (which included "kissing" scenes) in films and theatrical productions. Although a staunch Gandhian, Desai was socially conservative, pro-business, and in favour of free enterprise reforms, as opposed to Prime Minister Jawaharlal Nehru's socialistic policies.

Rising in Congress leadership, Desai was at odds with Prime Minister Nehru and his allies, and with Nehru's age and health failing, he was considered as a possible contender for the position of Prime Minister. Outflanked in the leadership contest after Nehru's death in 1964 by the Nehruvian Lal Bahadur Shastri, Desai remained content to build support within the ranks.

After Shastri's death in 1966, he contested for Prime Minister and fought a closely-contested election with Indira Gandhi. Desai obtained 169 votes but lost to Indira Gandhi who garnered 351.

Initially Desai stayed out of the Cabinet, biding his time. As the young Indira Gandhi s government became embroiled in controversy following a poor harvest, currency devaluation, and rising disenchantment in the country, Desai's influence grew in strength and he returned to the Cabinet in 1967. He demanded the powerful position as the Minister for Home Affairs, but he settled for the Ministry for Finance, with the added title of Deputy Prime Minister. Relations between Desai and the young Prime Minister were strained at best.

In 1969, Indira Gandhi and her allies engineered a major schism in the Congress Party, and her leftist supporters within the Congress Party formed the Congress (R), later to become the Congress (I) Party. Desai and the rest of the Congress establishment cohered to form the Congress (O) Party. But in the General Elections held in 1971, the Congress (O) was drubbed owing to Indira Gandhi's popularity as a wartime leader. Desai remained Leader of the Opposition that was viewed as a group of old men adhering to freedom-era legacies.

When Prime Minister Indira Gandhi was convicted in 1974 of wrongfully using government machinery for election work and corruption, Desai joined Jaya Prakash Narayan in organising mass protests throughout the country calling for her resignation. In a show of intolerance towards any sort of opposition, Indira Gandhi declared Emergency and had all the opposition leaders including Desai arrested in 1975.

When Indira called for elections in 1977, many opposition

groups, including the Congress (O), joined with longtime rivals, regional parties and blocs of rival ideologies to form the Janata Party. It won 356 seats, a near-absolute majority and for the first time since independence, the dominance of the ruling Congress Party was broken. He was later unanimously elected as Leader of the Janata Party in Parliament and was sworn in as the Prime Minister of India on March 24, 1977.

Desai led a fractious coalition government, and thus failed to achieve much owing to continuous in-wrangling and much controversy. With no party in leadership of the coalition, rival groups vied to unseat Desai. Controversial trials of prominent Congress leaders, including Indira Gandhi over Emergency-era abuses worsened the fortunes of his administration. Desai worked to improve relations with neighbours and arch-rivals Pakistan and restored normal relations with China, for the first time since the 1962 war. He communicated with Zia-ul-Haq and established friendly relations and diplomatic relations were also re-established with China. His government undid many amendments made to the constitution during emergency and made it difficult for any future government to impose national emergency.

Since India's first nuclear test in 1974, Desai kept India's nuclear reactors stating "they will never be used for atomic bombs, and I will see to it if I can help it". In 1977, the Carter administration sold India, heavy water and uranium for its nuclear reactors but required American on-site inspection of nuclear materials. Desai declined, seeing the American stance as contradictory, in light of its own nuclear arsenal.

In 1979, Charan Singh pulled out of the Janata Party, forcing

Desai to resign from office and retire from politics at the age of 83. He lived in Bombay, and died at the age of 99. He had been honoured much in his last years as the last great living freedom-fighter of his generation.

Morarji Desai was a strict follower of Mahatma Gandhi's principles and a moralist. Morarji Desai had described the RAW as the praetorian guard of Indira Gandhi and had promised to stop all activities of the RAW after becoming prime minister. B. Raman, the former head of the Counter-Terrorism Division of India's external intelligence agency, the Research and Analysis Wing (R&AW),reveals that, in an unguarded moment, Indian prime minister Morarji Desai indiscreetly told Pakistani dictator Zia ul-Haq that he was aware of Islamabad's nuclear schemes.

Morarji Desai was a true Gandhian follower, social worker, institutional builder and great reformer. He was Chancellor of Gujarat Vidyapith (university established by Mahatma Gandhi). Even during office of Prime Minister he was used to visit and stay in Vidyapith during month of October. He was exemplify simple and was used to write post card himself even when he hold office of P.M. Sardar Patel deputed him to conduct meetings in Kaira district farmers which finally turned to be AMUL Cooperative movement. During his rule, he withdrew intervention in Public Distribution System and rationing shops were literally lost due to cheap sugar and oil available in the market.

Morarji Desai died on 10 April 1995.

CHAUDHARY CHARAN SINGH

SHRI CHAUDHARY CHARAN SINGH (23 December 1902 – 29 May 1987) was the sixth Prime Minister of the Republic of India, serving from 28 July 1979 until 14 January 1980. Shri Charan Singh was born in 1902 at Noorpur in Meerut district of Uttar Pradesh, in a middle class peasant family. He graduated in science in 1923, and did his post-graduation from Agra University in 1925. Also trained in law, he set up practice at Ghaziabad. He shifted to Meerut in 1929 and later joined the Congress.

He was first elected to the U.P. Legislative Assembly in 1937 from Chhatrauli, and represented the constituency in 1946, 1952, 1962 and 1967. He became Parliamentary Secretary in Pandit Govind Ballabh Pant's Government in 1946 and worked in various departments such as Revenue, Medical and Public Health, Justice, Information etc.

Charan Singh entered politics as part of the Independence Movement. After independence he became particularly notable in the 1950s for opposing and winning a battle against Nehru's socialistic and collectivist land use policies, for the sake of the Indian Farmer. Popular especially among his native Jat community, his political base was Western Uttar Pradesh and Haryana, where that community was dominant.

The leader of the Bharatiya Lok Dal, a major constituent of the Janata coalition, he was disappointed in his ambition to become Prime Minister in 1977 by Jayaprakash Narayan's choice of Morarji Desai. He settled at the time for the largely honorary post of Deputy Prime Minister of India. However, the internal stresses of the coalition's government caused him to leave the government with the former Lok Dal, after being promised by Mrs. Gandhi the support of the Congress Party on the floor of the House in any efforts to form a government.

He was sworn in as Prime Minister with the support of just 64 MPs. During his term as Prime Minister the Lok Sabha never met. The day before the Lok Sabha was due to meet for the first time the Indian National Congress withdrew their support from his Bharatiya Lok Dal Government. Choudhary Charan Singh resigned and fresh elections were held six months later. He continued to lead the Lok Dal in opposition till his death in 1987, when he was succeeded as party president by his son Ajit Singh. His association with the causes dear to farming communities in the North caused his memorial in New Delhi to be named *Kisan Ghat.* The university of Meerut city in Uttar Pradesh India, is named after him (Chaudhary Charan Singh University).

In February 1937 he was elected to the Legislative Assembly of Uttar Pradesh (United Provinces) at the age of 34. In 1938 he introduced an Agricultural Produce Market Bill in the Assembly which was published in the issues of The Hindustan Times of Delhi dated 31 March 1938. The Bill was intended to safeguard the interests of the farmers against the rapacity of the traders. The Bill was adopted by most of the States in India, Punjab being the first state to do so in 1940.

Charan Singh followed Mahatma Gandhi in non-violent struggle for independence from the British Government, and was imprisoned several times. In 1930 he was sent to jail for 6 months by the British for contravention of the salt laws. He was jailed again for one year in November 1940 for individual Satyagraha Movement. In August 1942 he was jailed again by the British under DIR and released in November 1943.

In 1952, he became the Revenue Minister of state of Uttar Pradesh, the most populous state in independent India. He was dedicated to enforcing and implementing the provisions of the Zamindari Abolition and Land Reform Act of which he was the major architect. It has been argued by leading political scientists that success of Indian Democracy lies in successful implementation of this reform. Pakistan on the other hand did not have similar reforms, and the power is concentrated amongst the few powerful landlords or Zamindar who run their lands as their private fiefdom, and use their influence to further their wealth.

Charan Singh opposed Nehru on his Soviet Style Economic reform. Charan Singh was of the opinion that cooperative farms would not succeed in India. Being a son of a farmer, Charan Singh opined that the right of ownership was important to the farmer in remaining a cultivator. Charan Singh's political career suffered due to his open criticism of Nehru's economic policy. In 1950's, no one questioned Nehru in India.

In June 1951, he was appointed Cabinet Minister in the State and given charge of the Departments of Justice and Information. Later he took over as the Minister for Revenue and Agriculture in the Cabinet of Dr. Sampurnanand in 1952. When he resigned in April 1959, he was holding charge of the Department of Revenue and Transport.

In Shri C.B. Gupta's Ministry he was Minister for Home and Agriculture (1960). Shri Charan Singh served as Minister for Agriculture and Forests (1962-63) in Smt. Sucheta Kripalani's Ministry. He gave up the Department of Agriculture in 1965 and assumed charge of the Local Self-government department in 1966.

In Shri C.B. Gupta's Ministry he was Minister for Home and Agriculture (1960). Shri Charan Singh served as Minister for Agriculture and Forests (1962-63) in Smt. Sucheta Kripalani's Ministry. He gave up the Department of Agriculture in 1965 and assumed charge of the Local Self-government department in 1966.

Charan Singh left the Congress party in 1967, and formed his own political party. He had two short stints as Chief Minister of Uttar Pradesh in 1967, and later in 1970. In 1975, he was jailed again, but this time by then Indian Prime Minister Indira Gandhi, daughter of his former rival Nehru. She had declared the state of 'Emergency' and jailed all her political opponents. The Indian populace voted her out, and the opposition party, of which Chaudhary Charan Singh was a senior leader came into power. He served as Deputy prime minister and home minister in Janata government headed by Morarji Desai. He became Prime Minister of India in 1979. His speech to the nation on India's Independence Day (August 15, 1979) was very prophetic in which he identified Pakistan's nuclear ambition as a major threat to India. He also mentioned that Indian labour laws had to be refined if India were to become competitive in world economy. He also opened high level diplomatic relations with Israel, which Indira Gandhi's government which took office following the 1980 elections curtailed.'

Charan Singh passed away on May 29, 1987. He was survived by his wife, Gayatri Devi, five daughters (Satya, Vedvati, Gyanvati, Saroj and Sharda) and one son, Ajit Singh.

Chaudhary Charan Singh led a simple life and spent his spare time reading and writing. He was the author of several books and pamphlets, including 'Abolition of Zamindari', 'Co-operative Farming X-rayed', 'India's Poverty and its Solution', 'Peasant Proprietorship or Land to the Workers' and 'Prevention of Division of Holdings Below a Certain Minimum'.

RAJIV GANDHI

SHRI RAJIV GANDHI was born on August 20, 1944, in Bombay. He was an Indian politician who served as the sixth prime minister of India from 1984 to 1989. He took office after the 1984 assassination of his mother, then Prime Minister Indira Gandhi, to become the youngest Indian Prime minister at the age of 40. His grandfather was the Indian independence leader Jawaharlal Nehru, who would become India's first Prime Minister after independence. His parents moved to New Delhi from Lucknow. His father, Feroze Gandhi, became an M.P., and earned a reputation as a fearless and hard-working Parliamentarian. Rajiv Gandhi spent his early childhood with his grandfather in the Teen Murti House, where Indira Gandhi served as the Prime Minister's hostess. He briefly went to school at Welham Prep in Dehra Dun but soon moved to the residential Doon School in the Himalayan foothills. There he made many lifelong friendships and was also joined by his younger brother, Sanjay. After leaving school, Shri Gandhi went to Trinity College, Cambridge, but soon shifted to the Imperial College (London). He did a course in mechanical engineering. He really was not interested in 'mugging for his exams', as went on to admit later.

It was clear that politics did not interest him as a career. According to his classmates, his bookshelves were lined with volumes on science and engineering, not works on philosophy, politics or history. Music, however, had a pride of place in his interests.

He liked Western and Hindustani classical, as well as modern music. Other interests included photography and amateur radio. His greatest passion, however, was flying. No wonder then, that on returning home from England, he passed the entrance examination to the Delhi Flying Club, and went to the obtain a commercial pilot's licence. Soon, he became a pilot with Indian Airlines, the domestic national carrier.

At Cambridge, he met and fell in love with an Italian student Sonia Maino, who was there to learn English. Sonia's family opposed the match, but Sonia came to India with Rajiv and they were married in 1968. Gandhi began working for Indian Airlines as a professional pilot while his mother became Prime Minister in 1966. He exhibited no interest in politics and did not live regularly with his mother in Delhi at the Prime Minister's residence. In 1970, his wife, Sonia gave birth to Rahul, his first child, and in 1972, Priyanka, his second child and daughter. Theirs was a very private life despite the surrounding din and bustle of political activity.

But his brother Sanjay's death in an air crash in 1980 changed that. Pressures on Shri Gandhi to enter politics and help his mother, then besieged by many internal and external challenges, grew. He resisted these pressures at first, but later bowed to their logic. He won the by-election to the Parliament, caused by his brother's death, from Amethi in U.P.

In November 1982, when India hosted the Asian Games, the commitment made years earlier to build the stadia and other infrastructure was fulfilled. Shri Gandhi was entrusted with the task of getting all the work completed on time and ensuring that the games themselves were conducted without any hitches or flaws. In fulfilling this challenging task, he first displayed his flair for quiet efficiency and smooth coordination. At the same time, as General Secretary of the Congress, he started streamlining and energising the party organisation with equal diligence. All these qualities came to the fore later in far more testing and trying times.

For no one could have ascended to power - becoming both Prime Minister and Congress President - in more tragic and tormenting circumstances than Shri Gandhi did in the wake of his mother's brutal assassination on 31 October, 1984. But he bore the awesome burden of personal grief and national responsibility with remarkable poise, dignity and restraint. During the month long election campaign, Shri Gandhi travelled tirelessly from one part of the country to the other, covering a distance equal to one and a half times the earth's circumference, speaking at 250 meetings in as many places and meeting millions face to face.

A modern-minded, decisive but undemonstrative man, Shri Gandhi was at home in the world of high technology. And, as he repeatedly said, one of his main objectives, besides preserving India's unity, was to propel it into the twenty-first century.

Prime Minister Rajiv Gandhi began leading in a direction significantly different from Indira Gandhi's socialism. He improved bilateral relations with the United States - long strained owing to Indira's socialism and close friendship with the USSR - and expanded economic and scientific cooperation. He increased government support for science and technology and associated industries, and reduced import quotas, taxes and tariffs on technology-based industries, especially computers, airlines, defence and telecommunications. He introduced measures significantly reducing the *License Raj* - allowing businesses and individuals to purchase capital, consumer goods and import without red-tape and bureaucratic restrictions. In 1986, Rajiv announced a national education policy to modernize and expand higher education programs across India. Rajiv Gandhi was the founder of Jawahar Navodaya Vidyalaya System in the year 1986. Rajiv Gandhi can be called the father of telecom revolution. His efforts created MTNL in 1986 and the public call offices, better known as PCOs, helped spread telephones in the rural areas. The work that he did then laid the foundation for a telecom boom in 1990s.

Rajiv authorized an extensive police and Army campaign to contain terrorism in Punjab. A state of martial law existed in the Punjab state, and civil liberties, commerce and tourism were greatly disrupted. There are many accusations of human rights violations by police officials as well as by the militants during this period. It is alleged that even as the situation in Punjab came under control, the Indian government was offering arms and training to the LTTE rebels fighting the Government of Sri Lanka. The Indo-Sri Lanka Peace Accord was signed by Rajiv Gandhi and the Sri Lankan President J.R.Jayewardene, in Colombo on July 29, 1987. The very next day, on July 30, 1987, Rajiv Gandhi was assaulted by a Sinhalese naval cadet named Vijayamunige Rohana de Silva, while receiving honor guard. Though the embarrassed Sri Lankan President J.R. Jayewardene initially attempted to pass off the bizarre assault as "Rajiv tripped a little and slightly lost his balance", Rajiv Gandhi while enroute to New Delhi asserted to J.N. Dixit who was in charge of arranging that disastrous visit, "What is all this nonsensical speculation.

Of course, I was hit." Rajiv's government suffered a major setback when its efforts to arbitrate between the Government of Sri Lanka and the LTTE rebels backfired.

Rajiv's finance minister, Vishwanath Pratap Singh uncovered compromising details about government and political corruption, to the consternation of Congress leaders. Transferred to the Defence ministry, Singh uncovered what became known as the Bofors scandal, involving tens of millions of dollars - concerned alleged payoffs by the Swedish Bofors arms company through an Italian businessman and Gandhi family associate, Ottavio Quattrocchi, in return for Indian contracts. Upon the uncovering of the scandal, Singh was conspicuously dismissed from office, and later from Congress membership. Rajiv Gandhi himself was later personally implicated in the scandal, when the investigation was continued by Narasimhan Ram and Chitra Subramaniam of *The Hindu* newspaper, shattering his image as an honest politician, however, he was cleared over this allegation in 2004.

V. P. Singh's image as an exposer of government corruption made him very popular with the public, and opposition parties united under his name to form the Janata Dal coalition. In the 1989 elections, the Congress suffered a major setback. With the support of Indian communists and the Bharatiya Janata Party, V. P. Singh and his Janata Dal formed a government.

Rajiv Gandhi became the Leader of the Opposition, while remaining Congress president. While some believe that Rajiv and Congress leaders influenced the collapse of V. P. Singh's government in 1990 by promising support to Chandra Shekhar, a high-ranking leader in the Janata Dal, sufficient internal contradictions existed, within the ruling coalition, especially over the controversial reservation issue, to cause a fall of government.

Rajiv's Congress offered outside support briefly to Chandra Sekhar, who became Prime Minister. But this support was withdrawn in 1991 and fresh elections were announced.

The Indo-Sri Lanka Peace Accord signed was opposed by the then Sri Lankan Prime Minister Ranasinghe Premadasa and was forced to accept it due to pressure from then President Junius Richard Jayewardene. In January 1989 Premadasa was elected President and on a platform that promised that the Indian Peace Keeping Force (IPKF) leave within three months. In the 1989 elections both the Sri Lanka Freedom Party and United National Party wanted the IPKF to withdraw and they got 95% of the vote.The police action was unpopular in India as well, especially in Tamil Nadu as India was fighting the LTTE Tamil separatists.

Rajiv Gandhi refused to withdraw the IPKF, believing that the only way he could succeed in ending the civil war was to politically force Premadasa and militarily force the LTTE to accept the accord. Meanwhile in December 1989 Indian elections V.P.Singh became the Prime Minister and completed the pullout. The IPKF operation cost over 1100 Indian soldiers lives and cost over 2000 crores.

In 1985, Supreme court of India gave a judgement in favour of a Muslim divorcee Shah Banu that her husband should give alimony to her. Muslim fundamentalists in India treated it as an encroachment in Muslim Personal Law and protested against it. Prime Minister, Rajiv Gandhi, agreed to their demands and cited the gesture as an example of "secularism". In 1986, the Congress (I) party, which had an absolute majority in Parliament at the time, passed an act that nullified the Supreme Court's judgment in the Shah Bano case. The Shah Bano case generated tremendous heat in India. It proved that fundamentalist minorities can exert pressure on government and judicial decisions. The mainstream media disapproved of the decision. The opposition reacted strongly against the Congress party's policies (which, according to BJP, reflect "Pseudo-secularism".)

The case has led to Muslim women receiving a large, one-time payment from their husbands during the period of iddat, instead of a maximum monthly payment of 500 Rs (around 10 US dollars per month) - an upper limit which has since been removed. Cases of women getting lump sum payments for lifetime maintenance are becoming common.

Rajiv Gandhi's last public meeting was at Sriperumbudur on May 21, 1991, in a village approximately 30-miles from Chennai, Tamil Nadu. The assassination of Rajiv Gandhi, occurred as a result of a suicide bombing in Sriperumbudur, Chennai, in Tamil Nadu, India on 21 May 1991.

The Rajiv Gandhi Memorial was built at the site recently and is one of the major tourist attractions to the small industrial town.

AT THE UNITED NATIONS GENERAL ASSEMBLY. NEW YORK, JUNE 9, 1988

WE are approaching the close of the twentieth century. It has been the most bloodstained century in history. Fifty -eight million perished in two World Wars. Forty million more have died in other conflicts. In the last nine decades, the ravenous machines of war have devoured nearly one hundred million people. The appetite of these monstrous machines grows on what they feed. Nuclear war will not mean the death of a hundred million people. Or even a thousand million. It will mean the extinction of four thousand million: the end of life as we know it on our planet Earth. We come to the United Nations to seek your support. We seek your support to put a stop to this madness.

Humanity is at a crossroads. One road will take us like lemmings to our own suicide. That is the path indicated by doctrines of nuclear deterrence, deriving from traditional concepts of the balance of power. The other road will give us another chance. That is the path signposted by the doctrine of peaceful coexistence, deriving from the imperative values of nonviolence, tolerance and compassion.

In consequence of doctrines of deterrence, international relations have been gravely militarized. Astronomical sums are being invested in ways of dealing with death. Ever new means of destruction continue to be invented. The best of our scientific talent and the bulk of our technological resources are devoted to maintaining and upgrading this awesome ability to obliterate ourselves. A culture of armaments and threats and violence has become pervasive.

For a hundred years after the Congress of Vienna, Europe knew an uncertain peace based on a balance of power. When that balance was tilted - or more accurately, when that balance was perceived to have been tilted - Europe was plunged into an orgy of destruction, the like of which had never been known before and which spread to engulf much of the world. The unsettled disputes of the First World War led to the Second.

Humankind survived because, by today's standards, the power to destroy, which was then available was a limited power. We now have what we did not then have: the power to ensure the genocide of the human race. Technology has now rendered obsolete the calculations of war and peace on which were constructed the always dubious theories of the balance of power.

It is a dangerous delusion to believe that nuclear weapons have brought us peace. It is true that in the past four decades, parts of the world have experienced an absence of war. But a mere absence of war is not a durable peace. The balance of nuclear terror rests on the retention and augmentation of nuclear armories. There can be no ironclad guarantee against the use of weapons of mass destruction. They have been used in the past. They could be used in the future. And, in this nuclear age, the insane logic of mutually assured destruction will ensure that nothing survives, that none lives to tell the tale, that there is no one left to understand what went wrong and why. Peace which rests on the search for a parity of power is a precarious peace. If we can understand what went wrong with such attempts in the past, we may yet be able to escape the catastrophe presaged by doctrines of nuclear deterrence.

There is a further problem with deterrence. The doctrine is based on the assumption that international relations are frozen on a permanently hostile basis. Deterrence needs an enemy, even if one has to be invented. Nuclear deterrence is the ultimate expression of the philosophy of terrorism: holding humanity hostage to the presumed security needs of a few.

There are those who argue that since the consequences of nuclear war are widely known and well- understood, nuclear war just cannot happen. Neither experience nor logic can sustain such dangerous complacency. History is full, of miscalculations. Perceptions are often totally at variance with reality. A madman's fantasy could unleash the end. An accident could trigger a chain reaction, which inexorably leads to doom. Indeed, the advance of technology has so reduced the time for decisions that, once activated, computers programmed for Armageddon pre-empt human intervention and all hope of survival. There is, therefore, no comfort in the claim of the proponents of nuclear deterrence that everyone can be saved by ensuring that in the event of conflict, everyone will surely die.

The champions of nuclear deterrence argue that nuclear weapons have been invented and therefore, cannot be eliminated. We do not agree. We have an international convention eliminating biological weapons by prohibiting their use in war. We are working on similarly eliminating chemical weapons. There is no reason on principle why nuclear weapons too cannot be so eliminated. All it requires is the affirmation of certain basic moral values and the assertion of the required political will, underpinned by treaties and institutions, which insure against nuclear delinquency.

The past few years have seen the emergence of a new danger: the extension of the nuclear arms race into outer space. The ambition of creating impenetrable defenses against nuclear weapons has merely escalated the arms race and complicated the process of disarmament. This has happened in spite of the grave doubts expressed by leading scientists about its very feasibility. Even the attempt to build a partial shield against nuclear missiles increases the risk of nuclear war. History shows that there is no shield that has not been penetrated by a superior weapon, nor any weapon for which a superior shield has not been found. Societies get caught in a multiple helix of escalation in chasing this chimera, expending vast resources for an illusory security while incurring the risk of certain extinction.

The new weapons being developed for defense against nuclear weapons are part of a much wider qualitative arms race. The development of the so-called "third generation nuclear weapons" has opened up ominous prospects of their being used for selective and discriminate military operations. There is nothing more dangerous than the illusion of limited nuclear war. It desensitizes inhibitions about the use of nuclear weapons. That could lead, in next to no time, to the outbreak of full—fledged nuclear war.

There are no technological solutions to the problems of world security. Security can only come from our asserting effective political control over this self-propelled technological arms race. We cannot accept the logic that a few nations have the right to pursue their security by threatening the survival of humankind. It is not only those who live by the nuclear sword who, by design or default, shall one day perish by it. All humanity will perish.

Nor is it acceptable that those who possess nuclear weapons are freed of all controls while those without nuclear weapons are policed against their production. History is full of such prejudices paraded as iron laws: that men are superior to women; that the white races are superior to the colored; that colonialism is a civilizing mission, that those who possess nuclear weapons are responsible powers and those who do not are not.

Alas, nuclear weapons are not the only weapons of mass destruction. New knowledge is being generated in the life sciences. Military applications of these developments could rapidly undermine the existing convention against the military use of biological weapons. The ambit of our concern must extend to all means of mass annihilation.

New technologies have also dramatically expanded the scope and intensity of conventional warfare. The physical destruction, which can be carried out by full-scale conventional war, would be enormous, far exceeding anything known in the past. Even if humankind is spared the agony of a nuclear winter, civilization and civic life as we know it would be Irretrievably disrupted. The range, precision and lethality of conventional weapons is being vastly increased. Some of these weapons are moving from being 'smart' to becoming 'intelligent'. Such diabolical technologies generate their own pressures for early use, thus increasing the risk of the outbreak of war. Most of these technologies are at the command of the military blocs. This immensely increases their capacity for interference, intervention and coercive diplomacy.

Those of us who do not belong to the military blocs would much rather stay out of the race. We do not want to accumulate arms. We do not want to augment our capacity to kill. But the system, like a whirlpool, sucks us into its vortex. We are compelled to divert resources from development to defense to respond to the arsenals, which are constructed as a sideshow to great power rivalries. As the nature and sophistication of threat to our security increase, we are forced to incur huge expenditure on raising the threshold of our defences.

There is another danger that is even worse. Left to ourselves, we would not want to touch nuclear weapons. But when tactical considerations, in the passing play of great power rivalries, are allowed to take precedence over the imperative of nuclear non-proliferation, with what leeway are we left?

Even the mightiest military powers realize that they cannot continue the present arms race without inviting economic calamity. The continuing arms race has imposed a great burden on national economies and the global economy. It is no longer only the developing countries who are using disarmament to channel resources to development. Even the richest are beginning to realize that they cannot afford the current levels of the military burden they have imposed upon themselves. A genuine process of disarmament, leading to a substantial reduction in military expenditure, is bound to promote the prosperity of all nations of the globe. Disarmament accompanied by coexistence will open up opportunities for all countries, whatever their socio-economic systems, whatever their levels of development.

The technological revolutions of our century have

created unparalleled wealth. They have endowed the fortunate with high levels of mass consumption and widespread social welfare. In fact, there is plenty for everyone, provided distribution is made more equitable. Yet, the possibility of fulfilling the basic needs of nutrition and shelter, education and health remains beyond the reach of vast millions of people in the developing world because resources which could give fulfillment in life are pre-empted for death.

The root causes of global insecurity reach far below the calculus of military parity. They are related to the instability spawned by widespread poverty, squalor, hunger, disease and illiteracy. They are connected to the degradation of the environment. They are enmeshed in the inequity and injustice of the present world order. The effort to promote security for all must be underpinned by the effort to promote opportunity for all the equitable access to achievement. Comprehensive global security must rest on a new, more just, more honourable world order.

When the General Assembly met here last in Special Session to consider questions of disarmament, the outlook was grim. The new cold war had been revived with full force. A new programme of nuclear armament had been set in motion. As a result, during the years that followed, fear and suspicion cast a long shadow over all disarmament negotiations. Humankind was approaching the precipice of nuclear disaster.

Today, there is a new hope for survival and for

peace. There is a perceptible movement away from the precipice. Dialogue has been resumed. Trust is in the air.

How has this transformation occurred? We pay tribute to the sagacity of the American and Soviet leaderships. They have seen the folly of nuclear escalation. They have started tracing the outlines of a pattern of disarmament. At the same time, we must recognise the role of countless enlightened men and women all over the world, citizens of the non-nuclear weapon States as much as of the nuclear weapon States. With courage, dedication and perseverance they kept the candle burning in the enveloping darkness. The Six-Nation Initiative voiced the hopes and aspirations of these many millions. At a time when relations between the two major nuclear weapon states dipped to their nadir, the Six Nations-Argentina, Greece, India, Mexico. Sweden and Tanzania refocused world attention on the imperative of nuclear disarmament. The appeal of May 1984, issued by Indira Gandhi, Olof Palme and their colleagues, struck a responsive chord. Negotiations stalled for years began inching forwards. The process begun in Geneva has led to Reykjavik, Washington and Moscow.

We have all welcomed the ratification of the INF Treaty concluded between General Secretary Gorbachev and President Reagan. It is an important step in the right direction. Its great value lies in its bold departure from nuclear arms limitation to nuclear disarmament. We hope there will be agreement soon to reduce strategic nuclear arsenals by 50 per cent. The process should be carried forward to the total elimination of nuclear weapons. Only then will we be able to look back and say that the INF Treaty was a truly historic beginning. India believes it is possible for the human race to survive the second millennium. India believes it is also possible to ensure peace, security and survival into the third millennium and beyond. The way lies through concerted action. We urge the international community to immediately undertake negotiations with a view to adopting a time -bound Action Plan to usher in a world order free of nuclear weapons and rooted in nonviolence.

We have submitted such an Action Plan to this Special Session on Disarmament of the United Nations General Assembly. Our Plan calls upon the international community to negotiate a binding commitment to general and complete disarmament. This commitment must be total. It must be without reservation.

The heart of our Action Plan is the elimination of all nuclear weapons, in three stages, over the next twenty-two years, beginning now. We put this Plan to the United Nations as a programme to be launched at once.

While nuclear disarmament constitutes the centerpiece of each stage of the Plan, this is buttressed by collateral and other measures to further the process of disarmament. We have made proposals for banning other weapons of mass destruction. We have suggested steps for precluding the development of new weapon systems based on emerging technologies. We have addressed ourselves to the task of reducing conventional arms and forces to the minimum levels required for defensive purposes. We have outlined ideas for the conduct of international relations in a world free of nuclear weapons.

The essential features of the Action Plan are:

First, there should be a binding commitment by all nations to eliminating nuclear weapons in stages, by the year 2010 at the latest.

Second, all nuclear weapon States must participate in the process of nuclear disarmament. All other countries must also be part of the process.

Third, to demonstrate good faith and build the required confidence, there must be tangible progress at each stage towards the common goal.

Fourth, changes are required in doctrines, policies and institutions to sustain a world free of nuclear weapons. Negotiations should be undertaken to establish a Comprehensive Global Security System under the aegis of the United Nations.

We propose simultaneous negotiations on a series of integrally related measures. But we do recognize the need for flexibility in the staging of some of these measures.

In Stage-I, the INF Treaty must be followed by a fifty per cent cut in Soviet and U.S. strategic arsenals. All production of nuclear weapons and weapons grade fissionable material must cease immediately.

A moratorium on the testing of nuclear weapons must be undertaken with immediate effect to set the stage for negotiations on a Comprehensive Test Ban Treaty.

It is already widely accepted that a nuclear war cannot be won and must not be fought. Yet, the right is reserved to resort to nuclear war. This is incompatible with a binding commitment to the elimination of nuclear weapons. Therefore, we propose that all nuclear weapons be leached of legitimacy by negotiating an International convention which outlaws the threat or use of such weapons. Such a convention will reinforce the process of nuclear disarmament.

Corresponding to such a commitment by the nuclear weapon States, those nations, which are capable of crossing the nuclear weapons threshold, must solemnly undertake to restrain themselves. This must be accompanied by strict measures to end all covert and overt assistance to those seeking to acquire nuclear weapons.

We propose that negotiations must commence in the first stage itself for a new Treaty to replace the NPT, which expires in 1995. This new Treaty should give legal effect to the binding commitment of nuclear weapons States to eliminate all nuclear weapons by the year 2010 and of all the non-nuclear weapon States to not cross the nuclear weapons threshold.

International law already bans the use of biological weapons. Similar action must be taken to ban chemical and radiological weapons.

The international community has unanimously recognised outer space as the common heritage of mankind. We must expand international cooperation in the peaceful use of outer space. The essential prerequisite for this is that outer space be kept free of all weapons. Instead, there are plans of developing, testing and deploying a Space weapons system. The nuclear arms race cannot be ended and reversed without a moratorium on such activity. It should be followed by an agreement to forestall the militarisation of outer space. This is also an indispensable condition for attaining the goal of comprehensive global security based on a nonviolent world order free of nuclear weapons.

The very momentum of developments in military technology is dragging the arms race out of political control. The race cannot be restrained without restraining the development of such technology. We need a system, which fosters technological development but interdicts its application to military purposes. The arms control approach has focused on the quantitative growth of arsenals. The disarmament approach must devise arrangements for controlling the continuous qualitative upgradation of nuclear and conventional weapons. To achieve this purpose, the essential requirement is increased transparency in research and development in frontier technologies with potential military applications. This requires a systematic monitoring of such developments, an assessment of their implications for international security, and widespread dissemination of the information obtained. There is also need for greater international cooperation in research into new and emerging technologies for these technologies to open on new vistas of human achievement. Here, let us recall the vision of an open world voiced by one of the most remarkable scientists of our time, Niels Bohr. In his Open Letter to the United Nations on June 9 1950, thirty-eight years ago today, he said:

"The very fact that knowledge itself is a basis for civilization points directly to openness as the way to overcome the present crisis."

By the closing years of the century, there must be a single integrated multilateral verification system to ensure that no new nuclear weapons are produced anywhere in the world. Such a system would also help in verifying compliance with the collateral and other disarmament measures envisaged in the Action Plan. It would serve as an early warning system to guard against violations of solemn international treaties and conventions.

Beyond a point, nuclear disarmament itself would depend upon progress in the reduction of conventional armaments and forces. Therefore, a key task before the international community is to ensure security at lower levels of conventional defence. Reductions must, of course, begin in areas where the bulk of the world's conventional arms and forces are concentrated. However, other countries should also join the process without much delay. This requires a basic restructuring of armed forces to serve defensive purposes only. Our objective should be nothing less than a general reduction of conventional arms across the globe to levels dictated by minimum needs of defence. The process would require a substantial reduction in offensive military capabilities as well as confidence building measures to preclude surprise attacks. The United Nations needs to evolve by consensus a new strategic doctrine of non-provocative defence.

The Plan for radical and comprehensive disarmament must be pursued along with efforts to create a new system of comprehensive global security. The components of such a system must be mutually supportive. Participation in it must be universal.

The structure of such a system should be firmly based on non-violence. When we eliminate nuclear weapons and reduce conventional forces to minimum defensive levels, the establishment of a non-violent world order is the only way of not relapsing into the irrationalities of the past. It is the only way of precluding the recommencement of an armaments spiral. Non-violence in international relations cannot be considered an Utopian goal. It is the only available basis for civilised survival, for the maintenance of peace through peaceful coexistence, for a new, just, equitable and democratic world order. As

Mahatma Gandhi said in the aftermath of the first use of nuclear weapons:

"The moral to be legitimately drawn from the supreme tragedy of the bomb is that it will not be destroyed by counter bombs, even as, violence cannot be destroyed by counter-violence. Mankind has to get out of violence only through non-violence."

The new structure of international relations must be based on respect for various ideologies, on the right to pursue different socio-economic systems, and the celebration of diversity. Happily, this is already beginning to happen. Post-war bipolarity is giving way to a growing realisation of the need for coexistence. The high rhetoric of the system of military alliances is gradually yielding to the viewpoint of the Nonaligned Movement.

Nonalignment is founded on the desire of nations for freedom of action. It stands for national independence and self-reliance. Nonalignment is a refusal to be drawn into the barren rivalries and dangerous confrontations of others. It is an affirmation of the need for self-confident cooperation among all countries, irrespective of differences in social and economic systems. Nonalignment is synonymous with peaceful coexistence. As Jawaharlal Nehru said:

'The alternative to co-existence is co-destruction."

Therefore, the new structure of international relations to sustain a world beyond nuclear weapons will have to be based on the principles of coexistence, the non-use of force, non-intervention in the internal affairs of other countries, and the right of every state to pursue its own path of development. These principles are enshrined in the Chapter of the United Nations, but they have been frequently violated. We must apply our minds to bringing about the institutional changes required to ensure their observance. The strengthening of the United Nations system is essential for comprehensive global security. We must resurrect the original vision of the United Nations. We must bring the United Nations Organisation in line with the requirements of the New World order.

The battle for peace, disarmament and development must be waged both within this Assembly and outside by the peoples of the world. This battle should be waged in cooperation with scientists, strategic thinkers and leader of peace movements who have repeatedly demonstrated their commitment to those ideals. We, therefore, seek their cooperation in securing the commitment of all nations and all peoples to the goal of a non-violent world order free of nuclear weapons.

The ultimate power to bring about change rests with the people. It is not the power of weapons or economic strength, which will determine the shape of the world beyond nuclear weapons. 'Mat will be determined in the minds and the hearts of thinking men and women around the world. For, as the Dhammapada of the Buddha teaches us:

"Our life if shaped by our mind; we become what we think. Suffering follows an evil thought as the wheels of a cart follow the oxen that draw It. Joy follows a pure thought like a shadow that never leaves. For hatred can never put an end to hatred; Love alone can. This is the unalterable law."

VISHWANATH PRATAP SINGH

SHRI VISHWANATH PRATAP SINGH born on June 25, 1931 at Allahabad. He was an Indian politician who was the 8th Prime Minister of India from 1989 to 1990. He is the son of Raja Bahadur Ram Gopal Singh. He was educated at Allahabad and Poona Universities. He was married to Smt. Sita Kumari on June 25, 1955 and has two sons. A scholarly man, he was the proud founder of Gopal Vidyalaya, Intermediate College, Koraon, Allahabad. He was the

President of the Students Union at Udai Pratap College, Varanasi in 1947-48 and was the Vice-President, Allahabad University Students Union. He actively participated in Bhoodan movement in 1957 and donated a well-established farm in village Pasna, District Allahabad.

Entering local politics in Allahabad in the Nehru era, V.P. Singh soon made a name for himself in the state Congress Party for his unfailing rectitude, a reputation that he would carry with him throughout his career.

He was the member of All India Congress Committee; Executive Body, Allahabad University, 1969-71 and Legislative Assembly, Uttar Pradesh 1969-71. He was the Whip, Congress Legislative Party, 1970-71; Member of Parliament (Lok Sabha), 1971-74; Union Deputy Minister of Commerce, October 1974-November 1976; Union State Minister of Commerce, November 1976-March 1977; Member of Parliament (Lok Sabha), January 3-July 26,1980.

He was the Chief Minister of Uttar Pradesh, June 9, 1980-June 28, 1982; Member, Legislative Council, Uttar Pradesh, November 21, 1980-June 14,1981; Member Legislative Assembly, Uttar Pradesh, June 15, 1981-July 16, 1983.

As a Union Minister of Commerce in January 29,1983, he also held additional charge of the Department of Supply in February 15,1983. He was the Member of Parliament (Rajya Sabha) in July 16, 1983; on September 1, 1984 he was elected President, Uttar Pradesh Congress Committee and on December 31, 1984 he became the Union Finance Minister.

During his term as Finance Minister, he oversaw the reduction of gold smuggling due to reducing gold taxes and the excellent tactic of giving the police a portion of the smuggled gold that they found. He also gave extra power to the Enforcement Directorate of the Finance Ministry, which is the wing of the ministry charged with tracking down tax evaders.

Following a number of high-profile raids on suspected evaders - including Dhirubhai Ambani - Rajiv was forced to sack him as Finance Minister, possibly because many of the raids were conducted on industrialists who had supported the Congress financially in the past. However, Singh's popularity was at such a pitch now that only a sideways move was possible, to the Defence Ministry.

Once ensconced in North Block, Singh began to investigate the notoriously murky world of defence procurement. After a while, word began to spread that Singh possessed information about the Bofors defence deal that could damage the Prime Minister's reputation. Before he could act on it, he was dismissed from the Cabinet and, in response, resigned his memberships in the Congress Party and the Lok Sabha.

Together with associates Arun Nehru and Arif Mohammed Khan, Singh floated an opposition party named the Jan Morcha. He was re-elected to Lok Sabha in a bye-election from Allahabad defeating Anil Shastri. On 11 October 1988, the birthday of the original Janata coalition's spiritual leader Jayaprakash Narayan, the Janata Dal was formed by merger of Jan Morcha, Janata Party, Lok Dal and Congress (S), in order to bring together all the centrist parties opposed to the Rajiv Gandhi government.

The Janata Dal fought the elections in 1989 after coming to an agreement with the right-wing Bharatiya Janata Party and the Communist Left Front that served to unify the anti-Congress vote under the banner of a grouping called the

National Front. The three Opposition groupings earned a simple majority in the Lok Sabha and decided to form a government. The Communists and the BJP refused to serve in the government, preferring to support it from outside.

In a dramatic meeting in the Central Hall of Parliament on the 1st of December, V.P Singh proposed the name of Devi Lal as Prime Minister, in spite of the fact that he himself had been clearly projected by the anti-Congress forces as the 'clean' alternative to Rajiv and their Prime Ministerial candidate. Devi Lal, a Jat leader from Haryana stood up and refused the nomination, and said that he would prefer to be an 'elder uncle' to the Government, and that Singh should be PM. This last part came as a clear surprise to Chandra Shekhar, the former head of the erstwhile Janata Party, and Singh's greatest rival within the Janata Dal. Shekhar, who had clearly expected that an agreement had been forged with Lal as the consensus candidate, stormed out of the meeting and refused to serve in the Cabinet. Singh held office for slightly less than a year, from December 2, 1989 - November 10, 1990.

He faced his first crisis within few days of taking office; terrorists kidnapped the daughter of his Home Minister, Mufti Mohammad Sayeed (Ex Chief Minister of Jammu and Kashmir). His government caved into the demand for releasing militants in exchange; partly to end the storm of criticism that followed, he shortly thereafter appointed Jagmohan, a controversial former bureaucrat, as Governor of Jammu and Kashmir, on the insistence of the BJP, who were concerned that an insufficiently hard line was being taken with the separatist element in the state. Jagmohan subsequently inflamed opinion in the Valley when he ordered troops to fire on the funeral procession of the unofficial head of Kashmiri Islam, the Mirwaiz, and shortly thereafter the Kashmir insurgency began in earnest. In contrast, in Punjab, Singh replaced the hardline Siddhartha Shankar Ray as Governor with another former bureaucrat, Nirmal Kumar Mukarji, who moved forward on a timetable for fresh elections. Singh himself made a much-publicised visit to the Golden Temple to ask forgiveness for Operation Bluestar and the combination of events caused the long rebellion in Punjab to die down markedly in a few months. V.P. Singh withdrew the IPKF from Sri Lanka after he saw that Rajiv Gandhi's Sri Lanka policy was a miserable failure having cost over 1000 Indian soldiers' lives, over 5000 Sri Lankan Tamil lives and cost over 2000 crores; and the Sri Lankan leader Premadasa wanted the IPKF to leave in March 1990.

Singh himself wished to move forward nationally on social justice-related issues, which would in addition consolidate the caste coalition that supported the Janata Dal in North India, and accordingly decided to implement the recommendations of the Mandal Commission which suggested that a fixed quota of all jobs in the public sector be reserved for members of the historically disadvantaged so-called *Other Backward Classes*. This decision led to widespread protests among the youth in urban areas in North India.

Meanwhile the BJP was moving its own agenda forward: in particular, the Ram Janmabhoomi agitation, which served as a rallying cry for several radical Hindu organisations, took on new life. The party president, Lal Krishna Advani, toured the northern states on a *rath* - a bus converted to look like a chariot - with the intention of drumming up support. Before he could complete it, by reaching the disputed site in Ayodhya, he was arrested on Singh's orders on the charges of disturbing the peace and fomenting communal tension. This led to the BJP's suspension of support to the National Front government. V.P.Singh faced the vote of confidence with a high moral ground that he stood for secularism ,that he saved the Babri Masjid at the cost of power and that basic principles were involved. But he lost the vote by 142-346.

Chandra Shekhar immediately seized the moment and left the Janata Dal with several of his own supporters to form the Samajwadi Janata Dal, or the Socialist People's Party. Although he had a mere 64 MPs, Rajiv Gandhi, the leader of the Opposition, agreed to support him on the floor of the House so he won a confidence motion and was sworn in as Prime Minister. He lasted only a few months before Gandhi withdrew support and fresh elections were called.

Singh decided against contesting the new elections and retired from active politics. He spent the next few years touring the country speaking about matters related to issues of social justice, and painting. In the Deve Gowda and I.K. Gujral governments of the late 1990s, Singh acted as a sort of elder statesman and advisor for the successors to the National Front coalition. He was diagnosed with cancer in 1998 and ceased his public appearances.

When his cancer went into remission in 2003, he once again became a visible figure, especially in the many groupings that had inherited the space once occupied by his Janata Dal. Ironically, his caste-based social justice policies had caused the rise of parties like the Bahujan Samaj Party that were formed around caste identities; his own brand of populist socialism was thus squeezed out of the electoral marketplace. To remedy this, he re-formed the Jan Morcha in 2005, and began the slow process of aggregation of smaller parties in the North with a view to contesting the Uttar Pradesh vidhan Sabha elections scheduled for 2007.

Singh was placed under arrest in Ghaziabad as he and his supporters were proceeding towards a hauling where prohibitory orders under Section 144 had been imposed to join the farmers agitating against the acquisition of land by the Anil Ambani-owned Reliance Industries and demanding adequate compensation.

Singh's medical treatment after vacating the Prime Minister's post is also controversial in the sense that it has costed the state exchequer crores of rupees for this treatment abroad as a former Prime Minister. The government imported a state-of-the-art dialysis machine just for Singh's use at the taxpayer's cost. No one else except him is allowed to use the machine thus deprieving the tax payers superior medical equipment bought from their tax money. He will remain controversial for this.

He died in 27 November 2008.

CHANDRA SHEKHAR

SHRI CHANDRA SHEKHAR was born on July 1, 1927, in a farmer's family in Ibrahimpatti - Ballia in eastern Uttar Pradesh. Chandra Shekar did his Master of Arts (MA) at Allahabad University. He was known as a firebrand in student politics. After graduation, he became active in socialist politics. He was President of the Janata Party from 1977 to 1988. He was an Indian politician who served as the 8th

Prime Minister of India, between 10 November 1990 and 21 June 1991.

Shri Chandra Shekhar was attracted to politics from his student days and was known as a fire-brand idealist with revolutionary fervour. After his Master's Degree in Political Science from Allahabad University (1950-51), he joined the Socialist Movement. He had the privilege of having been associated very closely with Acharya Narendra Dev. He was elected Secretary of the District Praja Socialist Party, Ballia. Within a year, he was elected Joint Secretary of the U.P. State Praja Socialist Party. In 1955-56 he took over as General Secretary of the U.P., State Praja Socialist Party.

He came under the spell of Acharya Narendra Dev, a fiery Socialist leader in the beginning of his political career. From 1962 to 1967, Shekhar belonged to the Rajya Sabha, the Upper house of the Parliament of India. As a Member of Parliament he made a mark by taking keen interest in espousing the cause of the downtrodden and pleading for policies for rapid social change. In this context, when he attacked the disproportionate growth of monopoly houses with State patronage, he came in conflict with the centres of power. He had a nationwide *padayatra* in 1984 to know the country better as he claimed which gave the jitters to Indira Gandhi, the then Prime Minister.

He came to be as 'Young Turk' leader for his conviction, courage and integrity in the fight against vested interested. He founded and edited YOUNG INDIAN, a weekly published from Delhi in 1969. Its editorial had the distinction of being among the most quoted ones of the time. During the Emergency (June 1975 to March 1977) YOUNG INDIAN had to be closed down. It resumed regular publication in February 1989. He is the Chairman of its

Editorial Advisory Board. Shri Chandra Sekhar has always stood against politics of personalities and has favoured politics of ideology and social change. This propelled him more towards Shri Jayaprakash Narayan and his idealist view of life during the turbulant days of 1973-75. He soon became a focal point of dissent within the Congress Party.

After his predecessor, V.P. Singh, resigned, he led a breakaway faction of the Janata Dal, known as Samajwadi Janata Party. The Indian National Congress decided to extend outside support to his government to avoid snap elections, and Shekhar held a bare majority, with both the Communist parties and the BJP.

The relationship crumbled quickly, as the Congress party accused him of spying on Rajiv Gandhi, the Congress Party leader at that time. The party then boycotted Parliament and as Shekhar's faction only had about 60 MPs, he resigned in a nationally televised address.

Shri Chandra Shekhar undertook a marathon walk (Padayatra) through the country from Kanyakumari in the deep South to Rajghat (Samadhi of Mahatma Gandhi) in New Delhi covering a distance of nearly 4260 kms from January 6, 1983 to June 25, 1983. The Padayatra was undertaken to renew rapport with the masses and to understand their pressing problems.

He has established about fifteen Bharat Yatra Centres in various parts of the country including Kerala, Tamil Nadu, Karnataka, Maharashtra, Madhya Pradesh, Gujarat, Uttar Pradesh and Haryana to train social and political workers for mass education and grassroot work in backward pockets of the country. He has been a Member of Parliament since 1962 except for a brief period from 1984 to 1989. In 1989 he successfully contested both from his home constituency,

Ballia, and the adjoining Maharajganj constituency in Bihar. He vacated the latter.

Holding the office of Prime Minister for only seven months, Shekhar resigned on March 6, 1991 after the Congress Party withdrew support to him. He remained in office until national elections could be held later that year. Shekhar was known for abiding by the parliamentary conventions and was honoured with the inaugural Outstanding Parliamentarian Award in 1995.

Chandra Shekhar was a member of the Lok Sabha, India's lower house of Parliament. He led Samajwadi Janata Party (Rashtriya), (Socialist People's Party (National)). Starting in 1977, he won election to the Lok Sabha 8 times from Ballia in eastern Uttar Pradesh. The only election that he lost was in 1984 against Mr. Jagganath Chaudhary of Congress(I).

Shekhar suffered from multiple myeloma, a form of cancer of the plasma cell. On May 3, 2007, he was hospitalised in critical condition after his condition had deteriorated.

Shekhar died at the age of 80 in New Delhi on July 8, 2007. He was survived by two sons, Pankaj and Neeraj.

P. V. NARASIMHA RAO

PAMULAPARTHI VENKATA NARASIMHA RAO was born on June 28, 1921 at Karimnagar. He was the 10th Prime Minister of the Republic of India, and led one of the most important administrations in India's modern history that oversaw major economic transformation and checked national security crises.

Rao's father was P. V. Ranga Rao. He belonged to a wealthy Telugu Brahmin family from a village called *Vangara (pedda)* in the Karimnagar district of Andhra Pradesh, India.

Rao studied at Osmania University and at the Universities of Mumbai and Nagpur where he obtained Bachelor's and Master's degrees in law. He was a polyglot and could speak 13 languages including Urdu, Marathi, Kannada, Hindi, Telugu and English with a fluency akin to a native speaker. His mother tongue was Telugu. In addition to seven Indian languages, he spoke English, French, Arabic, Spanish and Persian. Along with his cousin Pamulaparthi Sadasiva Rao, Rao edited a Telugu weekly magazine called *Kakatiya Patrika* from 1948 to 1955.

Rao was an active freedom fighter during the Indian Independence movement and joined full time politics after independence as a member of the Indian National Congress. Rao served brief stints in the Indian union cabinet (1962–1971) and as chief minister of the state of Andhra Pradesh (1971–1973).

A polyglot, He could speak 17 languages, including Urdu, Marathi, Hindi, Telugu and English with fluency akin to a native speaker. His mothertongue was Telugu. Along with Devulapalli Ramanuja He and Sri Kaloji Narayana Rao, a great human rights activist in India, P.V. edited a Telugu bi-weekly magazine called "Kakatiya" in his early 20's. His father's name was P. V. Ranga Rao. They belonged to a poor Brahmin family from a village called "Vangara(pedda)" in Karimnagar District of Andhra Pradesh, India.

He was an active freedom-fighter during India's indpendence movement, and after independence, he joined politics full time. He served brief stints in the cabinet (1962 - 1971) and chief ministries (1971 - 1973) for the state of Andhra Pradesh. When the Indian National Congress split in 1969, he remained loyal to Prime Minister Indira Gandhi, and stayed so during the national emergency (1974-1977).

He then rose to the national level in 1972 by serving in several ministries, most significantly home, defence and foreign affairs (1980 - 1984), in the cabinets of Indira Gandhi and Rajiv Gandhi. He was the first PM from South India and Andhra Pradesh.

After the assassination of Rajiv Gandhi and the general elections of 1991, He was chosen to lead the Congress party, and when the Congress won a plurality in parliament later that year He was invited to head a minority government. He was the first person outside the Nehru-Gandhi dynasty to serve as Prime Minister for five continuous years. He was also the first Prime Minister to lead a minority government for a full term (five years) and the first prime minister from southern India.

Narasimha Rao became Prime Minister in 1991. India's leftist economic policies had caused economic stagnation. In the early 1990's longtime leftist regimes such as USSR and China were in the process of liberalization.

He believed India would benefit from undertaking such an economic transformation. He appointed Manmohan Singh (India's PM since 2004) as Finance Minister to accomplish his goals.He provided the much needed political will and support to push economic reforms. India's economy grew by an average of 6.3% between 1991-2000, a growth rate that continues with a predicted rate of 6.7% for 2005 (source: IMF World Economic Outlook). His supporters have claimed that this rate of growth is the result of spending cuts, deregulation, and privatization that began under the He government.Rao picked conservative BJP leader Atal Behari Vajpayee to represent India in the World Disarmament Conference. Although they were opponents, Vajpayee's hardline pro-nuclear stance was in accordance with Rao's own views. Vajpayee later became the Prime Minister.

Apart from the balance-of-payments crisis in 2001, He faced two other large challenges during his time in office. The Himalayan state of Jammu and Kashmir faced increased terrorist activity during Rao's tenure.

It was soon discovered that training camps in Pakistan administered Kashmir for these militants previously directed at evicting the Soviet army from Afghanistan were now producing the same fighters who were infiltrating Kashmir. Pakistan was directly charged with sheltering, arming and supplying infiltrators. Hindu pilgrims and Sikh settlers were attacked, and thousands of Kashmiri Pandits were forced to leave their homes in the Kashmir valley. Violence rocked and shut downparts of Kashmir, which is heavily depended on tourism, and also struck major cities like Delhi and Mumbai. Similar terrorism spread into the northeastern states of Assam, Tripura and Nagaland.He's government introduced the Terrorism and Disruptive Activities Act, India's first anti-terrorism legislation, and sent the Indian Army into full swing to eliminate the infiltrators, but despite a heavy and largely successful Army campaign, the state descended into a security nightmare. Tourism and commerce were largely disrupted, and the people began living in fear of the terrorists and the Army. Special police units were often accused of committing excesses against prisoners, including torture and excessive detention. Rao was criticized but the state remained stable and largely secure.

The long-agitating VHP activists attacked the Babri Mosque in Ayodhya on 3 December 1992. The site is claimed to bethe birthplace of Lord Rama. The destruction of the mosque, which was carried through the international media, unleashed the most vicious communal violence in the nation's modern history. Muslims retaliated with rioting across the country, infuriated by the destruction of the mosque, and incited by some Hindu elements, and and almost every major city like Delhi, Mumbai, Kolkata, Ahmedabad, Hyderabad and Chennai struggled to hold back mobs.Although intensive police operations brought the country back to peace. He was heavily criticized for this traumatic tragedy.A strong earthquake in Latur, Maharashtra, also killed 10,000 people and displaced hundreds of thousands in 1994-1995.Despite the tragedies, He was applauded for using modern technology and resources to organize major relief operations to assuage the stricken peoples, and for schemes of economic reconstruction.He also energized the national nuclear security and ballistic missiles program, which ultimately yielded in the 1998 Pokhran nuclear tests. It is speculated that these tests were actually planned in 1995, during Rao's own tenure itself. He increased military spending, and set the Army on course to fight the emerging threat of terrorism and insurgencies, as well as Pakistan and China's nuclear potentials. He also made diplomatic overtures to Western Europe, the United States and China.

In the 1996 general elections Rao's Congress Party was badly defeated and he had to step down as Prime Minister. He retained the leadership of the Congress party until late 1996 after which he was replaced by Sitaram Kesri. According to Congress insiders who spoke with the media, Rao had kept an authoritarian stance on both the party and his government, which led to the departure of numerous prominent and ambitious Congress leaders during his reign. Some of them were: Narayan Dutt Tiwari, Arjun Singh, Madhavrao Scindia, Mamata Banerjee, G.K. Moopanar and P.Chidambaram.

Rao rarely spoke of his personal views and opinions during his 5-year tenure. After his retirement from national politics Rao published a novel called *The Insider.* The controversial book, which follows a man's rise through the ranks of Indian politics, resembled events from Rao's own life. Rao, however denied any connection.

Rao suffered a heart attack on 9 December 2004, and was taken to the All India Institute of Medical Sciences where he died 14 days later at the age of 83.

He was cremated with full state honors. His body was kept in state at the Jubilee Hall in Hyderabad.

ATAL BIHARI VAJPAYEE

SHRI ATAL BIHARI VAJPAYEE was born on December 25, 1924 in the erstwhile princely state of Gwalior (now a part of the Indian State of Madhya Pradesh). He was one of seven children of Shri Krishna Behari, a secondary school teacher and Hindu scholar. Shri Vajpayee's rise in public life is a tribute to both his political acumen and Indian democracy. Over the decades, he has emerged as a leader who commands respect for his liberal worldview and commitment to democratic ideals. Vajpayee graduated from Victoria College (now called Laximbai College) in Gwalior and went on to earn a master's degree in political science from Dayanand Anglo-Vedic (D.A.V.) College in Kanpur.

Vajpayee is a native of Gwalior in Madhya Pradesh state and has been active in Indian politics throughout his adult life.

He was one of the founding members of the Bharatiya Jana Sangh, a party linked to the Hindu organisation Rashtriya Swayamsevak Sangh (RSS), of which he was the president between 1968 and 1973.

He was first elected to the Parliament of India in 1957 and was the leader of the Jana Sangh political party up to the formation of the Janata Party in 1977.

He served as the Foreign Minister in the government of Morarji Desai from March 1977 to July 1979. In 1980, he left the Janata Party,and helped form the Bharatiya Janata Party (BJP).

He was leader of the BJP parliamentary party between 1980 and 1984, 1986 and between 1993 and 1996. He was the leader of the Opposition in the 11th Lok Sabha.

On October 13, 1999, he took charge as Prime Minister of India for the second consecutive term at the head of a new coalition government, the National Democratic Alliance. He was Prime Minister for a short period in 1996. He is the only Prime Minister since Pandit Jawaharlal Nehru to have become Prime Minister of India with two successive mandates.

He was the Prime Minister again from 1998 until May 19, 2004. A Hindi poet and an orator, known for his spellbinding eloquence, Vajpayee's first brush with nationalist politics was in his students days when he joined the Quit India Movement of 1942. A student of political science and law, it was in college that he developed a keen interest in foreign affairs, which he put to skillful use while representing India at various multilateral and bilateral fora.

Shri Vajpayee had embarked upon a journalist's career, which was cut short in 1951 when he joined the Bharatiya Jana Sangh, the fore-runner of today's Bharatiya Janata Party, the leading component of the National Democratic Alliance. He became the Minister for External Affairs in 1977 when the Janata Party formed the government.

An ardent champion of women's empowerment and social equality, Shri Vajpayee believes in a forward-looking, forward moving India, a strong and prosperous nation confident of its rightful place in the comity of nations. He stands for an India anchored in 5000 years of civilisational history, ever modernising, ever renewing, ever re-energising itself to meet the challenges of the next 1000 years.

India's second highest civilian honour, the Padma Vibhushan, was conferred upon him in recognition of his selfless dedication to his first and only love, India, and his more than half-a-century of service to society and the nation. In 1994, he was named India's 'Best Parliamentarian.' The citation read: "True to his name, Atalji is an eminent national leader, an erudite politician, a selfless social worker, forceful orator, poet and litterateur, journalist and indeed a multi-faceted personality…Atalji articulates the aspirations of the masses… his works ever echo total commitment to nationalism.

On October 13, 1999, he took charge as the Prime Minister of India for the second consecutive term as the head of a new coalition government - the National Democratic Alliance. He has completed his tenure of 5 years as the Prime Minister of India. Now, he is one of the most respected political leaders of India. He died on 16 August 2018 (aged 93).

AT THE BANQUET ORGANIZED AT LAHORE BY PAKISTAN PRIME MINISTER NAWAZ SHARIEF, DURING THE FORMER'S FEB 18-20 VISIT TO PAKISTAN.

Mr Prime Minister, friends, sisters and brothers:

AS we break bread together; a new century and a new millennium knocks on our doors. Fifty years of our independence have gone by. On one side there is pride and on the other regret. Pride because both the countries have been successful in retaining their independence; but regret because even after 50 years we have not liberated ourselves from the curse of poverty and unemployment.

I am grateful to you, Mr Prime Minister, for hosting this banquet in such a historic location. It was in this magnificent fort that Shahjahan was born; it is here than Akbar lived for over a decade.

My delegation and I are overwhelmed by the warmth

of your welcome, and the gracious hospitality extended to us. Mr Prime Minister, you have upheld the nobility of this fort and the tradition of the historic city of Lahore. On this occasion, I am reminded of the lines of the 11th century poet Mas'ud bin S'ad bin Salman.

'Shud dar gham 'Lohur rawanam Yarab! Yarab! Ki dar arzu-e anam Yarab!' (My soul goes out in longing for Lohur, O God! How I long for it)

Excellency, this is the first visit by an Indian prime minister to Pakistan in 10 years. I am delighted to be here. When I inspected the guard of honour and saw the beautiful panorama of the setting sun, I was overwhelmed by mixed feelings. It gave me joy that I was returning here after 21 years with the message of friendship. My regret is that we have spent so much time in mutual bitterness. It is unworthy of two nations the size of India and Pakistan to have wasted so much time in mutual ill-will.

Earlier when I came to Pakistan, I was alone. This time we have representatives from every section of Indian society.

The bus service between Lahore and Delhi is not a means only to ease travel from one country to another. The running of the bus between the two countries symbolises the desire of the people to improve relations and come together. Indeed, if this was only a bus made of metal, it would not have caused such excitement and expectations, not only in our two nations but all over the world.

It is our duty, Mr Prime Minister, to pursue the desires and wishes of our peoples; to develop, trust, confidence, amity and to create a solid structure for co-operation.

We have been encouraged that our interaction in recent months has focussed on issues which directly benefit the lives of our peoples. Our two countries have engaged within the composite dialogue process to work out mechanisms to ensure that humanitarian concerns are addressed quickly; that possibilities of economic and commercial co-operation such as sale of power are identified and pursued; that confidence-building measures are discussed and agreed upon. But this marks only a beginning. We will, together, give directions to our officials to accelerate what we have jointly set in motion.

We have also discussed those areas of relationship on which we do not see eye to eye. That is only inevitable. As we seek to resolve issues, we have to be conscious that there is nothing which cannot be solved through goodwill and direct dialogue. That is the only path.

I am convinced that there is nothing in our bilateral relations that can ever be resolved through violence. The solution of complex outstanding issues can only be sought in an atmosphere free from prejudice and by adopting the path of balance, moderation and realism. To those that preach, practice or foment violence, I have only one message: understand the simple truth of the path of peace and amity. That is why, as part of the composite dialogue process, we welcome sustained discussions on all outstanding issues, including Jammu and Kashmir. As we approach a new millennium, the future beckons us. It calls upon us, indeed demands of us, to think of the welfare of our children and their children, and of the generations that are yet to come.

I have brought but one message from India. There can be no greater legacy that we can leave behind than to do away with mistrust, to abjure and eliminate conflict, to erect an edifice of durable peace amity, harmony and co-operation. I am confident that through our combined efforts we will succeed in doing so, no matter how hard we have to work in achieving it.

Permit me to extend to you, Mr Prime Minister and to Begum Sahiba a most cordial invitation to visit India. Let me assure you that you will find in India a very warm welcome. We look forward to receiving both of you soon in India.

I express my best wishes for your progress and prosperity, for the establishment of durable peace and co-operation between India and Pakistan.

PRIME MINISTER'S ADDRESS TO THE NATION ON THE SUBJECT OF KARGIL, JUNE 7, 1999

My dear Countrymen.

You are well aware of the situation which has developed in Kargil.

It is a serious situation.

It is a situation fraught with danger.

It is a situation that has arisen from one simple fact the decision of Pakistan to cross the Line of Control, to send its men and materials to occupy and territory.

No government can tolerate such an incursion - our Government certainly will not. Countries the world over have recognized that we have the full right to evict these intruders from our soil. But for me and for my Government this is not just a matter of our having a tight. It is our duty to rid our sacred Motherland of every single intruder. For this reason, as you have seen, our armed forces have launched a major operation to drive them back. No one should entertain the slightest doubt: they shall not stop till they have completely attained their objective. No one shall stop them till they have done so. You know well that our relations with Pakistan, as with all our neighbours, were improving rapidly:

The Prime Ministers and other ministers of the two countries were in regular contact.

Dialogue among officials of the two countries was proceeding constructively, and satisfactorily.

Areas of cooperation had been identified, and, at various levels, plans were afoot to work together on each of them.

Most important, people-to-people contacts and exchanges had opened up as never before in fifty years, there had been an outpouring of goodwill on both sides.

In the midst of all this, regulars of Pakistan Army and infiltrators have been sent across. Fomenting insurgency here was heinous enough. But this time Army regulars have been sent. They have been sent to occupy our territory. And, having occupied it, to choke off our links with other parts of our country - in particular with Siachen and Ladakh. This step has been taken after a great deal of preparation. It was a pre-planned operation. It is a repudiation of the letter and spirit of the Lahore Declaration. It is a violation not just of one article of the Shimla Agreement, but an eight-fold violation of that solemn Agreement.

The Shimla Agreement binds each side to respect the territorial integrity sovereignty, and Independence of the other. The Clauses repeatedly or join that neither side shall use the threat of force or force to affect the territorial integrity of the other. The Agreement deals specifically with the Line of Control. It lays down that the line of control resulting from the cease-fire of December 17,1971 shall be respected by both sides. ~Furthermore, that ~Neither side shall seek: to alter it unilaterally~. The Agreement goes a step ahead and India wants peace. We are at peace with all other neighbors of ours. We were taking major steps with Pakistan also -- towards undoing the fifty-year history of bitterness. Our people desire it. Our Government is committed to it. We have traveled quite some distance for it.

I remain confident that the people of Pakistan too yearn for peace and harmony. They know the possible costs of hostilities -- of how these will push economic gains even further beyond the horizon. They know that in today's world whosoever launches aggression of any kind will get isolated in the international community.

Moreover both India and Pakistan are nuclear powers. Our responsibilities in this regard are all the greater.

Therefore, I once again urge the Government of Pakistan: undo the armed intrusion. We must hope, my countrymen, that even now reason will prevail, that those within Pakistan who see the folly of aggression will have their way. But till that happens, we have a job on our hands.

Our first thought, and our last thought must be for our jawans, for our airmen and our officers who are fighting back the intruders. I want each one of them to know: the entire country stands with you, every Indian is grateful to you. The whole operation has been thrust upon us. To ensure victory, you would not be wanting in your requirements.

Our jawans and officers are laying down their lives. Should we be continuing our petty squabbles at such a time? We should stand by them and avoid unnecessary debates. Let us use this occasion to learn from our defence forces; let us translate into our own conduct some of the discipline for which they are renowned.

The whole world is watching how our brave armed forces are defending the Motherland in hospitable hilly terrain and at grave risks to their lives. In this hour of crisis, we must maintain an equanimity and act with confidence.

We should not be disheartened by some momentary mishap. We must realise the gravity of the situation and emulate the fortitude with which our fighting men take such events in their stride :

Have confidence in the ability of our armed forces.

The armed forces shall accomplish this task and ensure that no one dares to indulge in this kind of misadventure in future.

Jai Hind.

PRIME MINISTER'S ADDRESS TO THE THREE SERVICE CHIEFS AND ARMY COMMANDERS JULY 10, 1999

'Operation Vijay' has given great 'Vijay' to the country. This is a historic moment for all of us. It is only befitting, therefore, that in these few brief sentences that I share with you, my first tribute and homage is to those brave soldiers and airmen of our country who fought, laid-down their lives or were wounded, to achieve this 'Vijay'. To them the nation owes an everlasting debt of gratitude.

I take this opportunity to also, unstintingly, place on record the great appreciation, indeed admiration that our entire nation has today for the outstanding valour, determination and military skill that has been demonstrated in 'Operation Vijay'. Out brave military has achieved one sterling success after another in these operations.

I know how impossible the terrain is. I also know, what great demands were placed on the sense of dedication of our troops who come from all states of our country. We asked of them to achieve extremely difficult tasks. These they fulfilled in more than abundant measure.

I share with the bereaved families their grief. I gave them a commitment that their welfare is my bounden duty.

'Operation Vijay" in the Kargil sector, of 1999, will go down in the annals of our military history as another outstanding example of the valour, discipline and dedication of our armed forces.

The enemy's, intrusion and aggression in Kargil has now been decisively turned back. Out military has achieved this. Most pockets have already been cleared. There, our troops are back on the LOC. The remaining pockets will also be cleared. Residual Pak forces will leave or be evicted from south of the LoC in the entire Kargil sector.

I offer you my heartiest congratulations, on my personal behalf, on behalf of my government, and on behalf of the entire nation. I also offer you the nation's great gratitude an admiration.

PRIME MINISTER VAJPAYEE' INDEPENDENCE DAY ADDRESS TO THE NATION ON AUGUST 15, 1999

Sisters, Brothers and Dear Children,

Accept my greetings on the sacred occasion of Independence Day. This is a day of hallowed remembrance for us. This is a day of dedication for us.

This year's Independence Day has special significance for all of us. The present century is coming to an end. The world will have entered the next century by the time of the next Independence Day.

As we stand at the sunset of the 20th century, and look back at the events of the era that has passed, we see the end of colonialism from Indian soil to be the most important development. Our great leaders, and many generations of our countrymen, waged a powerful struggle for independence. By doing so, they paved the way for the independence of other countries, too.

We pay our homage to those self-sacrificing and devoted leaders and patriots who struggled for freedom throughout their lives, and, when necessary, even laid down their lives as *aahuti* (offering) in the great *yagya* of freedom.

Come, all my countrymen, let us strive to become worthy heirs to those great leaders. We dedicate today's sacred day to their memory.

In the same way, I offer my condolences to the valiant jawans, officers and others belonging to the Army and the Air Force, who displayed magnificent heroism and the spirit of sacrifice in recapturing that part of our Motherland in Kargil from the enemy. All of us bow our heads in gratitude for those who were martyred in the Kargil war.

Almost all our countrymen have seen on television glimpses of the impossible summits, which our heroes overcame and pushed out the enemy. To gain victory at such heights is not only to surmount the sky-piercing peaks, it displays the full might of the nation. It is a symbol of the bravery of our Armed Forces.

How can we forget such heroes?

How can we forget those wounded soldiers whose only wish was: how fast can we get well and rejoin our battalion to repulse the enemy?

How can we forget the members of the families of those brave martyrs, who, on receiving the body of their beloved, said, "We do not have tears in our eyes, we have pride in our heart"?

How can we forget the mother whose lament was that she had had only one son, and therefore, could not send another to fight for our country?

I know that mere words of solace are not enough. We have to take concrete measures for the families of the martyrs and wounded soldiers so that they may live a life of comfort and dignity.

It has been said that we remember and honour soldiers during a war, and in the immediate aftermath. But as the days pass, we forget them. And it is a sad fact that many who sacrificed their life and limb in previous wars were often forgotten. I give you my personal pledge that this will not happen again.

This Red Fort and its world-renowned ramparts are not merely a geographical spot. The very heartbeat of India's freedom struggle is linked to this fort and its ramparts. In the First War of Independence of 1857, this is where Bahadur Shah Zafar was held a prisoner.

Netaji Subhash Chandra Bose made this very fort the target of his campaign in 1943 and, blowing the bugle of Independence, gave the stirring call to his countrymen: "*Dilli Chalo, Chalo Lal Kile*"

It is from this very fort that our first Prime Minister, Pandit Jawaharlal Nehru hoisted for the first time, the tricolour of Free India in 1947.

More than half a century has passed. Today, we stand at the threshold of a new era.

Come, let us enter this new era united in step and united in resolve.

When I addressed you from this rampart last year, there was uncertainty and cynicism in the atmosphere. It was being asked:

- Will we be able to withstand economic sanctions?
- To what extent will we be able to ward off the economic crisis, which had struck the Tiger economies of Southeast Asia?
- Will the Government be allowed to carry on its work? Today, speaking to a self-confident India, I declare:
- Sanctions have lost their effect. They have become a thing of the past. We have dealt with them in such a way that they hardly had any effect on our economy;
- We kept the South-east Asian economic crisis at bay;
- Yes, the Government was brought down, but the country was not. It continued to march ahead, fulfilling the mantra of *Charaiveti, Charaiveti* (Move on, Move on). The Government continued to discharge its duty.
- Most important, a war was imposed on us.

We have not just triumphed over difficulties, we

have achieved much. In spite of obstacles that were put in our way,

- Our National Income has grown by 6 percent;
- Having crossed 200 million tonnes, production of foodgrains is higher today than ever before;
- Food stocks are higher today than ever. For this our kisans deserve our felicitations. Our agricultural scientists are also worthy of our praise.
- Industrial production is reviving at an energetic pace;
- The new initiatives which have been taken in infrastructure have infused a new purposefulness right across the economy;
- At over 30 billion dollars our foreign exchange reserves are higher than ever before;
- The Sensex in the stock market has risen to record levels. In spite of Kargil, our companies have been able to increase their market value by over Rs. 200,000 crore.
- The off-take of cement for building houses is 22 percent higher than it has ever been;
- Facilities which were known only to the rich, to the few, and in our cities alone — insurance for their output, credit cards — are now available to, and are being taken advantage of by farmers and by others in our far-flung villages.

And we are stronger than ever. Pokharan has given us enviable strength and self-confidence. AGNI-2 has been tested — in the face of pressures — and will be integrated into our defence arsenal.

PSLV and INSAT 2-E have been launched. What a feat our scientists have accomplished: sending not just one, but three satellites on a single rocket far out into space, and placing each of them at the precise point in space, which had been fixed. This has been a magnificent achievement.

Yes, one thing has certainly come down. It is the rate of inflation. At 1.3 percent, this is the lowest rate in seventeen years.

There has also been a sea change in the way the world sees us. Last year we had taken a major step — Pokharan 2 — which was essential for our security, a step which had been contemplated for long but which could not be taken because of the pressures which were put on successive governments.

Some did not agree with our assessment. Some even sought to portray us as an irresponsible nation. However today, within a year, in the councils of the world, "India" is synonymous with "responsibility".

The world has seen that we will protect our national interest at all costs: whether it is in developing an atomic weapons capability, whether it is in developing missile-capability, whether it is in driving adversaries out of our land:

- The world has seen that we will withstand all pressures that are intended to keep us from taking the measures that we consider necessary in our national interest;

- Also the world has seen that whatever we will do will be for self-defence, never for aggression.

But the world has also seen that we are capable of doing so with utmost restraint, with utmost responsibility. These were the principles, which guided us when Pakistan forced the Kargil war on us. Our response was well-thought out. It was so effective that it left the enemy stunned.

The world today has well realized that we would do whatever is required to protect our country. The world has also understood that we would act with utmost responsibility and restraint even when so gravely provoked. This has raised the reputation of India in the international community.

The Lahore bus journey was taken to improve our relations with Pakistan. This made the world realize that we truly want peace and friendship. This journey was not a showpiece. It was a serious and well-considered move, which we made knowing fully well that there could be risks in it.

Our honesty made an impact on the international community. Later, when the bus to Lahore was taken to Kargil, it did not take much time for the world to realize that Pakistan not only violated the Shimla Agreement and the Lahore Declaration, but it also crossed the borders of trust and goodwill.

That is what turned the world's opinion. Pakistan stood completely isolated on the world stage. India received widespread support in the world for the first time.

I do hope that the people of Pakistan too will reflect on these events. We reached out to you with a message of friendship. What did we gain in return? Hundreds lost their lives. Relations were spoilt. The resources which ought to have been used for economic and social development were instead spent on war.

We need peace in order to raise the standard of living of the people in both countries. For peace, we need trust. Has trust increased on account of all that happened in Kargil, Does the path of armed intrusion lead to friendship?

Terrorists are being trained in Pakistan. Camps are being run for them. Hordes of terrorists are being sent into India. They are killing innocent people. They are targeting women and children. How can meaningful dialogue take place in this atmosphere?

Pakistan must realize that no problem can be resolved if it continues to promote terrorist activities. We shall not let the evil designs of terrorists succeed. Today, Punjab is free of terrorism. The people of Jammu and Kashmir are fed up with terrorism. Even Assam and the North-East are affected.

All of us want peace. People are worried about the future of their children.

Terrorism is a curse on the world. When it is combined with religious extremism, it becomes a graver danger to humanity. All of you are familiar with the saying "*Karela Aur Neem Chadha*" (The bitterness of Karela is further worsened by adding to it the bitterness of Neem.)

In our case, over thirty five thousand of our people have been killed by terrorists. Terrorism has become a big problem in many other parts of the world, too. It is obstructing the path of peace and development. Today, there is a need to mobilize world opinion against terrorism.

Today, on the occasion of Independence Day, India stands with full self-confidence. Our gaze is turned to the future. Our standing in the world has risen. Now, the people are not attracted by the controversies and narrow disputes of yesterday.

Throughout the war in Kargil, I was specially satisfied by two features.

- There was no communal tension anywhere in the country. Goodwill and brotherhood prevailed everywhere, including in Jammu and Kashmir. This must have despaired those who thought that riots would break out in India as soon as the spark of war is lit. Those who hatched the conspiracy of strife, must have been truly disillusioned. The people of all sections of society worked for India's success in the war. A powerful wave of patriotism traveled everywhere.

- When I went to Kargil and met our jawans, I saw our entire country there: soldiers from Nagaland,

> from Assam, from Tamil Nadu, from almost every state were fighting for the country. There was not the slightest distance between them on account of caste or religion or region.

This is the real India. We must make their oneness our own. We have to live for this India. We have to work for this India. And, if necessary, we have to lay down our lives for this India, as our brave jawans did.

Kargil has once again shown that whenever our patriotism is aroused, all of us stand as one with full confidence and determination, as a fist clenched in conviction. We face our challenges unitedly. Our adversaries should beware of this.

At the same time, there is an equally important lesson for us. Now that the crisis has been beaten back, do not unclench this fist of unity.

The battle is not over. New challenges are knocking at our doors. The patriotism that coursed through the veins of Indians should be made a permanent feature of our lives.

All of us remember the talisman Gandhiji gave us: when in doubt about what to do, he taught us, think of the least, of the most helpless man you have seen, ask yourself, "Will this step be in his interest?" he said, and you will see all your doubts melt away.

Kargil gives us a second talisman: As we contemplate a step, let us ask ourselves: "Is it worthy of the soldier who gave his life on those mountains? Does the impulse which lies behind it measure up to the spirit which filled that soldier as he fought to protect our Motherland?"

The challenges that confront us cannot be overcome only by the men on the frontiers doing their duty. There is a need for an organized and disciplined nation to stand behind them. We must defend our country and develop our society by keeping national interests utmost in our minds. If our economy is not strong, and if we are not self-reliant in important matters of national security, then we cannot successfully face external challenges.

All of us, wherever we may be, whatever work we may be doing, we should discharge our responsibilities well. We must never allow any limb of our nation or society to become weak.

It is clear from the effective way in which we have overcome our challenges and dealt with our difficulties, that we can do anything if we resolve to do it. What is needed is to take a pledge: that whatever we can do, we will now do.

I have a vision of India: an India free of hunger and fear, an India free of illiteracy and want.

I dream of an India that is prosperous, strong and caring. An India, that regains a place of honour in the comity of great nations.

- Come, let us build an India in which we have balanced development that benefits all regions and all sections of society. I note with regret that several regions in the country — including the North-Eastern States — have been the victims of unbalanced progress. The nation has an especially pressing obligation to bring the people of the North-East into the developmental mainstream.

- Come, let us build an India in which Dalits, Adivasis, and Backward Classes are not only freed from economic deprivation, but also enjoy the fruits of social justice. The path that will take us to this ideal is the path of *samata, mamata*, and *samajik samarasata*.

- Come, let us build an India in which our *nari shakti* — our women — are able to realize its full potential — from shaping the future of their families to shaping the future of the nation. It is our collective responsibility to empower them economically, socially, educationally and also politically. In this regard, I would like to see early passage of the legislation to reserve seats for women in Parliament and State Assemblies. We have already seen how women have given an excellent account of themselves wherever they have got an opportunity to serve in panchayats and other local bodies.

- Come, let us build an India in which the minorities fully enjoy the fruits of national development, while having full opportunities to contribute to it. Our country belongs to all. And all are entitled to equal and fair treatment in the eyes of the law and the Government. India, which is home to the great secular principle of *Sarva Panth Samabhav*, fully guarantees the religious freedom of all communities. It is a matter of immense pride for India that all the religions of the world have a harmonious co-existence here. Unity in Diversity is our priceless heritage.

It is also a matter of much satisfaction that the past year has seen a record low in communal violence.

- India is the largest democracy in the world. The tradition of democracy in our country is very old. When this Century opened, democracy was the preserve of just a handful of countries, and even in them it was limited to small sections of the people. Today there are just a handful who are still out of the pale of democracy. There is scarcely a country whose people do not aspire to it.

- Come, let us strengthen Indian democracy. Let us make it an ideal for other countries of the world. Let us transform our political democracy into economic and social democracy.

- Come, let us make India a nation of high achievers — in every sphere. In business and economy, in education, in science and technology, in arts and culture, and also in sports. Let us make India synonymous with "achievement", achievement of the kind that can be benchmarked globally. All of us are heartened by what our young men and women have achieved in recent times. The success stories of young Indians working abroad are making headlines almost every day. If young Indians can script such shining successes abroad, why shouldn't we create conditions for them to do so *right here?*

- Come let us together build a Parishrami Bharat, a Parakrami Bharat, a Vijayi Bharat.

To realize this vision, let us step out of the swamp of negativity.

Let us not be obsessed with the past. Face the future.

March with confidence towards the goal.

Turn from problems — to solutions.

Today, when the 20th century is coming to an end, and the 21st century is knocking at our doorsteps, let us draw inspiration from our glorious past and resolve to build an even more glorious future.

We are inheritors of an ageless culture and a proud civilization. Greatness is our past — and also our future.

Come, let us make good use of the natural and human resources of our Motherland, Bharat and make the 21st century, India's century.

Come, let all of us together raise our voice in saying:

Jai Hind,

Jai Hind,

Jai Hind.

H. D. DEVE GOWDA

SHRI HARADANAHALLI DODDEGOWDA DEVE GOWDA was the 12th Prime Minister of the Republic of India (1996–1997) and the 14th chief minister of the state of Karnataka (1994–1996). He was born on May 18, 1933 in Haradanahalli village of Holenarasipura taluk, Hassan District in Karnataka into a farming family. A Civil Engineering Diploma holder, Shri Deve Gowda plunged into active politics at the early age of 20 when, after completing his education, he joined the Congress Party in 1953 and remained a member till 1962. Coming from a middle class agrarian background and exposed to the hardships of farmer's life, young Gowda vowed to become a fighter who would take up the cause of poor farmers, under privileged and oppressed sections of society.

He won his first seat in the Karnataka state assembly in 1962, rising to become Karnataka's chief minister. In the late 1970s Deve Gowda rose in the Janata party and was an important figure in reuniting its successor, the Janata Dal party, after the original group splintered in 1980.

Deve Gowda was instrumental in attracting to the party divergent castes. When the Congress party was defeated in the 1996 general elections and Prime Minister P. V. Narasimha Rao resigned, Deve Gowda became prime minister of the United Front coalition government after BJP failed to form a government.

He was the President of Anjaneya Co-operative Society and later as a member of Taluk Development Board, Holenarasipura. In 1962, Deve Gowda contested from Holenarasipur constituency as an independent candidate for Karnataka Legislative Assembly elections and became an MLA. Later he was elected from the same constituency for three more consecutive terms: the fourth (1967-71), the fifth (1972-77), and the sixth (1978-83) Assemblies.

Later he resigned his membership of the Sixth Assembly on 22 November 1982. As a member of the Seventh and the Eighth Assembly, he served as the Minister of Public Works and Irrigation. He resigned from the Cabinet in 1987 in protest against insufficient allocation of funds for irrigation. His tenure as Irrigation Minister saw the switching on of many irrigation projects. He resigned from the Cabinet in 1987 protesting against insufficient allocation of funds for Irrigation.

A crusader for freedom and equality, he earned the wrath of the powers that be at the Centre in 1975-76, and was imprisoned during the days of emergency. Shri Deve Gowda utilised this period of forced rest to enrich his knowledge through exhaustive reading. This, and the interaction between him and other stalwarts of Indian politics who were also jailed during that period, helped him mould his personality and perspective. He was a much more seasoned and determined person when he emerged out of his confinement.

Elected to Parliament from Hassan Lok Sabha constituency in 1991, he was instrumental in bringing the problems of the State - especially of farmers - to the forefront. He earned respect for his forthright espousal of the plight of farmers, in Parliament. He also earned a name for practising and upholding the prestige and dignity and Parliament and its institutions.

He also became the President of Janta party twice at State level and President of State Janata Dal in 1994. He was the driving force behind the Janata Dal's rise to power in the State in 1994.

He was elected as the leader of the Janata Dal Legislative Party and on December 11, 1994 he assumed office as the 14th Chief Minister of Karnataka. He then contested as a candidate from Ramanagar Assembly constituency and won by a thumping majority.

His prolonged experience in active politics and his strong base at the grassroots level enabled him to plunge straightway into the task of tackling many problems faced by the State. His political acumen was tested again when he brought the Idgah Maidan issue at Hubli to the forefront. It was a ground that belonged to the minority community and was the butt of political controversy. Shri Gowda successfully brought about a peaceful solution to the issue.

In January 1995, Shri Gowda toured Switzerland and attended the Forum of International Economists. His tours to European and Middle Eastern countries were a testimony to his achievements as a dedicated politician. His tour to Singapore, which brought in the much needed foreign investment to the State, proved his business acumen.

Since the 70s, friends as well as foes have been commenting on his singular pre-occupation with politics and its processes. His politics, says Shri Gowda, is the politics of the people and he is happy when he is surrounded by people and is doing something for them.

Shri Gowda is known for giving patient hearing to all shades of opinions and is equally at home with the elite when they come calling. Affectionately called the 'son of the soil' (dharti ke lal), he has proved to be one of the most ardent supporters of liberalisation with a human face.

In 1989, his group of the Janata Party fared poorly in Karnataka winning just 2 of the 222 Assembly seats it contested; Shri Gowda himself tasting defeat for the first time in his career losing in both constituencies he contested. He is therefore, no stranger to the fickleness of political fortunes.

The defeat lent a sharper edge to his pursuit to regain lost honour and power, and spurred him to re-examine his own style of politics. He made friends in Karnataka and Delhi, and put aside his bitter feuds with political rivals. Shri Gowda is a person with a life style that is simple, a profile that is low, but assertive and effective.

Before his political initiation, Shri Gowda had been a contractor taking up minor works. The seven years that he spent as an Independent helped him observe party politics from outside. Ever a workaholic, he was always seen engrossed with books and periodicals in the legislature library.

His re-election in 1967 gave him more confidence and in 1969 when the Congress split, he joined the Congress (O) headed by Shri Nijalingappa, which was in power in Karnataka then. But Shri Gowda's big chance came after the rout of Congress (O) in the 1971 Lok Sabha elections. He emerged the leader of a truncated opposition hit by the Indira Gandhi wave. His leadership of the Third Front (a group of regional parties and Non-Congress and Non-BJP combine) led to his Prime Minister's job.

Deve Gowda resigned as the Chief Minister of Karnataka on 30 May 1996 to be sworn in as the 11th Prime Minister of India. He was noted as being the only Prime Minister who could not speak Hindi which is one of the national languages of India.

He is the president of the Janata Dal (Secular) (JD-S) political party in India and currently a member of Parliament (MP) representing his home town Hassan district in Karnataka. The JD-S had formed a coalition with the Congress party government led by Dharam Singh. There are allegations of nepotism owing to his two children H.D. Revanna and H.D. Kumaraswamy being powerful in this government. Revanna had served as a minister in that government.

In January 2006, H.D. Kumaraswamy, son of Deve Gowda took support of around 40 JD(S) MLAs and the BJP to bring down the Dharam Singh led coalition government. This prompted Devegowda to resign from his post as party president owing moral responsibilities for failing to save the Dharam Singh government.

However, in February 2006, he withdrew his resignation and suspended 40 JD(S) MLAs of the Karnataka Legislative Assembly, including his son and Chief Minister H D Kumaraswamy, from the primary membership of the party. It was speculated that the entire political fiasco was orchestrated by Deve Gowda to elevate his son to the political summit. Recently, Mr. Gowda has openly supported his son's move to align with the BJP, provided it stuck to a common development agenda.

He has also suggested that he would be willing to coordinate the BJP-led alliance on a national level, going against his previous adamant stance against dealing with the BJP. The stance led a split in his party, the Janata Dal.

INDER KUMAR GUJRAL

SHRI INDER KUMAR GUJRAL was the 13th Prime Minister of the Republic of India from April 1997 to March 1998. Son of Late Shri Avtar Narain Gujral and Late Smt. Pushpa Gujral, Shri Gujral is M.A., B.Com. Ph.D. & D.Litt. (Hons. Causa). He was born at Jhelum (in undivided Punjab) on 4th December 1919. He and Smt. Shiela Gujral were married on May 26, 1945. Shri Gujral belongs to a family of freedom fighters: both his parents participated in the freedom struggle in Punjab. At the young age of eleven, he himself actively participated in the freedom struggle in 1931 and was arrested and severely beaten by the police for organising movement of young children in the Jhelum town. In 1942, he was jailed during the Quit India Movement.

In the tumultuous days of June 1975, he was minister of Information and Broadcasting. On June 12,1975, the Allahabad high court gave a verdict that Prime Minister Mrs. Indira Gandhi used unfair means in elections of 1971 and termed her election null and void.

There were reports that her son, Sanjay Gandhi brought people from neighboring state of Uttar Pradesh in a number of trucks to Delhi and held massive demonstrations in support of the Prime Minister. It was also reported that Sanjay wanted Gujral to give coverage of the rallies on state run television and radio. However Gujral refused to obey Sanjay Gandhi, who did not hold any constitutional post. Many people believe that it was the reason why Gujral was replaced by Vidya Charan Shukla as minister of Information and Broadcasting.

Later, Gujral was appointed India's ambassador to Russia. By the time of Indira Gandhi's return to power in 1980,as the Indian envoy to Moscow, Gujral persuaded her to express opposition to the Soviet Union's 1979 invasion of Afghanistan. That was a break from India's earlier record of supporting Soviet military ventures in Hungary and Czechoslovakia, and it led Mrs. Gandhi to privately inform Soviet leader Leonid I. Brezhnev that the Kremlin had blundered in Afghanistan.

Gujral left the Congress Party in the mid-1980s and joined the Janata Dal. The Dal was a third-party with mainly socialist leanings and regional bases. In 1989 elections, Gujral was elected from Jallandhar parliamentary constituency of Punjab. He served as Minister of External Affairs in V.P.Singh cabinet. The issue he had to deal with as External Affairs Minister was Iraq's invasion of Kuwait and the subsequent events that led to first gulf war of January 1991.In 1989 V P Singh sent him to Srinagar to seal the deal with the kidnappers in case of 1989 kidnapping of Rubaiya Sayeed.

As India's representative, he personally met with Iraq's Saddam Hussein. His hug with Hussein during the meeting remains a matter of controversy. In 1991 mid-term parliamentary elections, Gujral contested from Patna constituency in Bihar against Janata Dal(S) candidate and then Finance Minister Mr. Yashwant Sinha. However the election was countermanded following complaints of large scale irregularities.

In 1992,Gujral was elected to Rajya Sabha and remained a key Janata Dal leader.After 1996 elections, when United Front government was formed at the center under the leadership of H.D.Deve Gowda, he was again named Minister of External Affairs of India. During his second tenure as Minister of External Affairs, he propounded his 'Gujral Doctrine' which called for better relations with neighbors. With Gujral at the helm of Ministry of External Affairs, India resolved long standing dispute over Ganga water sharing with Bangladesh.

Before becoming the Prime Minister of India in April 1997, he served the country as Union Minister or Minister of State holding different portfolios in the Ministries of Communications and Parliamentary Affairs, Information & Broadcasting, Works & Housing, Planning and Ministry of External Affairs.

The Congress party, which was supporting the United Front government from outside decided to withdraw support, which led to the collapse of the government in April 1997.In order to avoid elections, compromise was reached and the Congress party agreed to support another United Front government under new leader, provided its concerns like not being consulted before taking important decisions and being marginalized were addressed. The United Front elected Gujral as new leader and he was sworn in as Prime Minister on April 21,1997.

Gujral inherited the bitterness between Congress party and the United Front from his predecessor, HD Deve Gowda. However he adroitly maintained good relations with the Congress party that was supporting his government from outside. Within a few weeks in office, Prime Minister Gujral faced a trouble, not from the Congress party but within his own Janata Dal. The CBI asked for the permission from the governor of Bihar Mr. AR Kidwai to prosecute the state chief minister Lalu Prasad Yadav in a corruption case related with purchase of fodder for the cattle.

The state governor granted the permission for the prosecution of the chief minister and demand for the resignation of Yadav was raised both from within and out of the United Front. However Laloo Prasad Yadav sternly rejected the demand. Prime Minister Gujral just exhorted Yadav to step down without actually taking any action against his government.

When Gujral transferred the CBI director Mr. Joginder Singh, who was investigating the case against Yadav, many people considered this as an attempt on the part of Prime Minister to protect Yadav. When Laloo Prasad Yadav felt that he no longer enjoyed commanding position in Janata Dal, he left the party and formed his own 'Rashtriya Janata Dal' (RJD) on July 3, 1997. Out of 45 Janata Dal members of parliament, 17 left the party and supported Yadav. However, the new party continued in the United Front and Gujral's government was saved from immediate danger.

Prime Minister Gujral continued in the office for over 11 months, including 3 months as caretaker Prime Minister. During this time, he attempted to improve relations with Pakistan, reform the aging institutions of government and promote pro-growth economic policies to bring the country out of the 1997 Asian financial crisis, which had left it stagnant. But the fractious, corrupt and unstable coalition politics were too big a hurdle.

One of the most controversial decisions of his government was recommendation of President's rule in Uttar Pradesh, following unruly scenes in the state assembly on October 21,1997. The BJP government headed by Kalyan Singh sought vote of confidence when the violence and unruly scenes took place in the assembly. However President K.R. Narayanan refused to sign the recommendation and sent it back to the government for reconsideration. Gujral government decided not to pursue the matter further and let Kalyan Singh's government continue in Uttar Pradesh.

In early November 1997, parts of interim report of Jain Commission inquiring into the conspiracy aspect of Rajiv Gandhi assassination case were leaked to the press. Reportedly, the Jain Commission had indicted the political party, DMK (Dravid Munnetra Kazhagam) for tacitly supporting the LTTE, which was responsible for Rajiv Gandhi's assassination. The DMK was part of the ruling coalition at the center and the Union Cabinet had ministers belonging to the DMK. The Congress party first demanded the tabling of the report on the floor of the parliament. The report was tabled on 19 November 1997. When it was confirmed that the Jain Commission had in fact held the DMK responsible for supporting the LTTE, the Congress party demanded that the ministers belonging to the DMK be dropped. There was exchange of letters between Congress President Sitaram Kesri and Prime Minister Gujral. However, Gujral refused to budge. In a public function in Calcutta on November 23,1997, he gave a hint of what was to follow saying 'mid-term elections are around the corner'.The Congress party finally withdrew support to his government on November 28,1997. Gujral resigned following the withdrawal of support by the congress party. As no alternative government could be formed, the only alternative was mid-term elections, as Gujral had foreseen.

The Gujral Government was sadly in the mire of a very fractious, chaotic stage in the evolution of democracy in India. It failed to achieve any particular goal towards national progress and public welfare despite being headed by an able administrator with clean image, Gujral. However, I.K. Gujral had the distinct privilege and honor of leading the country in its 50th year of independence, a year of pride and major celebrations of the country's diversity, vibrant cultural fabric, achievements of the past five decades, and of course, honoring the national freedom struggle and its veterans.

The elections were held in February-March 1998.Gujral contested again from Jallandhar constituency in Punjab with the support of Akali Dal. The Akali Dal, though a part of BJP-led coalition opted to support Gujral because during his Prime Ministerial tenure, Gujral declared that the central government will share the expenses on stamping out terrorism in Punjab during 1980s and early 1990s, along with the state government of Punjab. That eased the strain on economy of Punjab to a great extent and the Akali Dal decided to support Gujral. Gujral defeated Umrao Singh of the Congress party by over 131,000 votes. In the 12th Lok Sabha, Gujral actively opposed the BJP-led coalition government.

In a debate in Lok Sabha on May 29,1998, he pointed out some of the drawbacks of the government in handling of the nuclear tests conducted at Pokhran. He also opposed the government's decision to impose President's rule in Bihar. However Gujral actively supported Prime Minister Vajpayee's visit to Lahore in February 1999 and signing of Lahore Declaration with Pakistan Prime Minister, Nawaz Sharif. On April 19,1999, when the BJP-led government sought vote of confidence on the floor of the Lok Sabha after the withdrawal of support by AIADMK, Gujral opposed the government.

He did not contest 1999 elections and retired from active politics. Shri Gujral has been a writer and commentator on National and International Affairs, as well as theatre. He speaks fluent Urdu, and spends part of his leisure time writing Urdu couplets, a poetic form that traces back to India's Mogul emperors. His brother Satish Gujral is a prominent painter and architect. Gujral and his wife Sheila Gujral, a poet and the author of several books have two sons; Naresh and Vishal Gujral.

In 2004, his son Naresh Gujral unsuccessfully contested with an Shiromani Akali Dal seat from Jalandhar, Punjab constituency in the Indian General Elections.

He died in 2012 at the age of 92, following hospitalization due to a lung infection.

DR. MANMOHAN SINGH

SHRI MANMOHAN SINGH is an Indian economist, academic, and politician who served as the 14th Prime Minister of India from 2004 to 2014. Dr. Manmohan Singh is rightly acclaimed as a thinker and a scholar. He is well regarded for his diligence and his academic approach to work, as well as his accessibility and his unassuming demeanour.

Dr. Manmohan Singh was born on September 26, 1932, in a

village in the Punjab province of undivided India. Dr. Singh completed his Matriculation examinations from the Panjab University in 1948. His academic career took him from Punjab to the University of Cambridge, UK, where he earned a First Class Honours degree in Economics in 1957. Dr. Singh followed this with a D.Phil in Economics from Nuffield College at Oxford University in 1962. His book, "India's Export Trends and Prospects for Self-Sustained Growth" was an early critique of India's inward-oriented trade policy.

Dr. Singh's academic credentials were burnished by the years he spent on the faculty of Punjab University and the prestigious Delhi School of Economics. He had a brief stint at the UNCTAD Secretariat as well, during these years. This presaged a subsequent appointment as Secretary General of the South Commission in Geneva between 1987 and 1990.

In 1971, Dr. Singh joined the Government of India as Economic Advisor in the Commerce Ministry. This was soon followed by his appointment as Chief Economic Advisor in the Ministry of Finance in 1972. Among the many Governmental positions that Dr. Singh has occupied are Secretary in the Ministry of Finance; Deputy Chairman of the Planning Commission; Governor of the Reserve Bank of India; Advisor of the Prime Minister; and Chairman of the University Grants Commission.

In what was to become the turning point in the economic history of independent India, Dr. Singh spent five years between 1991 and 1996 as India's Finance Minister. His role in ushering in a comprehensive policy of economic reforms is now recognized worldwide.

Among the many awards and honours conferred upon Dr. Singh in his public career, the most prominent are India's second highest civilian honour, the Padma Vibhushan (1987);

the Jawaharlal Nehru Birth Centenary Award of the Indian Science Congress (1995); the Asia Money Award for Finance Minister of the Year (1993 and 1994); the Euro Money Award for Finance Minister of the Year (1993), the Adam Smith Prize of the University of Cambridge (1956); and the Wright's Prize for Distinguished Performance at St. John's College in Cambridge (1955). Dr. Singh has also been honoured by a number of other associations including by the Japanese Nihon Keizai Shimbun.

Dr. Singh has represented India at many international conferences and in several international organizations. He has led Indian Delegations to the Commonwealth Heads of Government Meeting in Cyprus (1993) and to the World Conference on Human Rights in Vienna in 1993.

In his political career, Dr. Singh has been a Member of India's Upper House of Parliament (the Rajya Sabha) since 1991, where he was Leader of the Opposition between 1998 and 2004. Singh served as Governor of the Reserve Bank of India from 1982 to 1985, and was hand picked as finance minister in cabinet of then Prime Minister Narasimha Rao in 1991.

Singh became leader of opposition in uppder house of Indian Parliament, and stayed with the Congress Partyduring a major split in 1999, when three senior Congress leaders objected to Sonia Gandhi's rise as Congress President. Being touted as the Congress choice for the PM's job, Gandhi had become a target of nationalists who objected to her Italian birth.

An alliance led by the Congress Party won a surprisingly high number of seats in the Parliamentary elections of 2004. The Left Front decided to support a coalition government led by the Congress Party from the outside. Sonia Gandhi was elected leader of the Congress Parliamentary Party and was expected to become the Prime Minister. In a surprise move, she declined to accept the post and instead nominated Dr. Singh.

He secured the nomination for prime minister on May 19, 2004 when the then President A.P.J. Abdul Kalam officially asked him to form a government. Although most expected him to head the Finance Ministry himself, he entrusted the job to P. Chidambaram.

His appointment is notable as it comes 20 years after India witnessed significant tensions between the Indian central government and the Punjabi Sikh community. After Congress Party Prime Minister Indira Gandhi, the mother-in-law of Sonia Gandhi, ordered central government troops to storm the Golden Temple (the holiest site of Sikhism) in Amritsar, Punjab to quell a separatist movement, she was assassinated by her Sikh bodyguards.

Singh's image is generally regarded as intellectual, honest but cautious, attentive to working class people (on whose votes he was elected), and technocratic. Although legislative achievements have been few and the Congress-led alliance is routinely hampered by conflicts, Singh's administration has focused on reducing the fiscal deficit, providing debt-relief to poor farmers, extending social programs and advancing the pro-industry economic and tax policies that have launched the country on a major economic expansion course since 2002.

Singh has been the image of the Congress campaign to defuse religious tensions and conflicts and bolster political support from minorities like Muslims, Christians and Sikhs.The Prime Minister's foreign policy has been to continue the new peace process with Pakistan initiated by his predecessor, Atal Bihari Vajpayee. Exchange visits by top leaders from both countries have highlighted this year, as has reduced terrorism and increased prosperity in the state of Kashmir.

His government has endeavored to build stronger relations with the United States, the People's Republic of China and European nations. The Government suffered a setback when it lost the support of a key ally, several African Union members, for its bid for a permanent membership to the U.N. Security Council with veto privileges. One of the biggest achievements of Manmohan Singh's Government has been a nuclear deal between India and the U.S.A. Under Dr. Singh, an economist and Finance minister P. Chidambaram, India's economic growth has continued, with the GDP growing at a very fast rate. This has resulted in India becoming a trillion dollar economy.

Dr. Singh and his wife Mrs. Gursharan Kaur have three daughters. Dr. Singh visited China on 14th January, 2008 and extended successfully friendship and trade economy with that country. In May, 2009, the U.P.A. again won the General Elections with securing 206 seats on it's own and Dr. Manmohan Singh once again became Prime Minister of India for the second term.

PM'S ADDRESS AT THE UNITED NATIONS GENERAL ASSEMBLY SEPTEMBER 23, 2004, NEW YORK

"Allow me to congratulate you on your election as President of the 59th Session of this august assembly. May I assure you of India's full support in ensuring its success.

As we gather here on the 60th year of the United Nations – we might perhaps pause to reflect on the fate of the ideas and ideals of the international community that animated its creation. The post-war generation had already become aware that the world, which had emerged from the ashes of the global war could no longer be a peaceful world unless the underlying forces of conflict were addressed effectively by the entire community of nations as a collectivity. Nations therefore were united together to make the world a safer and more peaceful place, a world in which a free people could together pursue a destiny of shared prosperity.

The impulse behind the creation of global institutions nearly sixty years ago has become even more pressing reality today. If we look around us, the single most defining characteristic of our contemporary world is the global, transnational character of the many challenges we confront, whether these are in the realm of international security or development. Virtually every major issue that we face as nation states, has both a domestic as well as a transnational dimension. It is becoming increasingly apparent as never before that unless we fashion a global response, based on a meaningful consensus, to these challenges, we would not succeed in creating a world that truly manifests the ideals of the United Nations.

Terrorism is one such challenge for which many of us have paid an unacceptable price. We shall not forget that three years ago, it was this great city that witnessed the single most horrendous terrorist act in human history. About three weeks ago, the world saw another brutal act of terror, in Russia, which took the lives of hundreds of innocent civilians, including a large number of young children. Terrorism exploits the technologies spawned by globalisation, recruits its foot soldiers on ideologies of bigotry and hatred, and directly targets democracies. And yet it is a sad reality that international networks of terror appear to co-operate more effectively among themselves that the democratic nations that they target. We speak about co-operation, but seem often hesitant to commit ourselves to a truly global offensive to root out terrorism, with the pooling of resources, exchange of information, sharing of intelligence, and the unambiguous unity of purpose that is required. This must change. We do have a global coalition against terrorism. We must now give it substance and credibility, avoiding selective approaches and political expediency.

Let me turn to other major challenges that we face today, such as the proliferation of weapons of mass destruction. There is an increasing reliance on restrictive regimes and the use of punitive action to confront this threat to international peace and security. While India is firmly opposed to proliferation and has an impeccable record in this respect, we believe that it is only a global consensus of willing nations that would ultimately prove to be truly effective in this regard.

The Chemical Weapons Convention is a good model to follow in respect of other weapons of mass destruction including nuclear weapons. It is through representative institutions rather than through exclusive clubs of privileged countries that we can address global threats posed by the proliferation of weapons of mass destruction and their means of delivery.

As far back as in 1988, Prime Minister Rajiv Gandhi had outlined a series of specific steps in an Action Plan, whose central proposition remains valid even today – that progressive steps towards the elimination of weapons of mass destruction must be based on a balance of obligations between those who possess such weapons and those who do not. It is quite evident today that a global discourse is required for evolving a more cooperative and consensual international security order. India believes that this consensus must differentiate between States whose actions strengthen non-proliferation and those that weaken the realisation of its objectives.

Let me now turn to the central theme for the vast majority of UN members; the challenge of development and the eradication of mass poverty. Globalisation has undoubtedly brought enhanced effectiveness and efficiency in the functioning of our economies. It has integrated market places, higher standards of living and a revolution in global connectivity. But, there is also the phenomenon of widening economic disparities, both within and among countries. Connectivity also means that the people are painfully aware – in real time – of how far and how fast they are falling behind in their relative conditions of living. Development today is no longer a function of domestic resources and national policies alone. It is a process that is vitally linked to the international economic environment that the developing countries face.

The international community must find ways to contract these circles of exclusion. We need to find innovative sources of financing and access to new technologies that are necessary to assist those who are on the margins of globalisation. Just as prosperity cannot be sustained by being walled in, poverty cannot be banished to some invisible periphery. Development, therefore, must return to the centre of the global discourse. We must evolve equitable and rule-based regimes to manage global trade, investment flows and movement of services. Four years ago, at our Millennium Summit, we adopted ambitious global development goals, but it is a matter of concern that we have already fallen behind in their implementation.

While globalisation has generated new challenges, it has also given us new technologies to deal with these massive challenges. The world faces looming pandemics such HIV/AIDS, but it today also possesses remedies and skills that can rid the world of this scourge. We face problems of environmental degradation in many parts of our planet, but we also have available safe and environment-friendly technologies. Many countries are beset by problems of hunger and malnutrition, but we possess modern techniques of food production and processing to make a hunger-free world a credible and realistic dream. Although our excessive dependence on hydrocarbons raises concerns about the long-term availability of energy, and about the security of supplies, technology has made available many environmentally sound alternatives. What we lack however, is a truly global concert and a mobilisation of the international community to overcome these massive challenges.

The experience of the decades since the inception of the United Nations demonstrates the great significance of democracy as an instrument for achieving both peace and prosperity. While it is gratifying that the frontiers of democracy have expanded dramatically, in the last decade and a half, they still exclude significant numbers. Only a few months ago, in India's 14th General Elections, our country went through the largest exercise of popular will in the world. I can therefore assert with confidence the importance of national articulations in global forums, truly reflecting the democratically expressed will of their people. We choose to overlook the absence of democracy in too many cases for reasons of political expediency.

Democracy's representative nature validates the commitments we take on as countries; it should also determine the manner in which the architecture of international institutions evolves. For what is required for the international community to successfully deal with global challenges, whether they be security challenges, economic challenges, or challenges in the sphere of the environment are the existence of international institutions and a culture of genuine multilateralism. The United Nations and its specialised agencies are the only instruments available for responding effectively to the challenges we face collectively. But what is missing, is our sustained commitment to democratising the functioning of the United Nations.

It is common knowledge that the UN is often unable to exert an effective influence on global economic and political issues of critical importance. This is due to what may be called as 'democracy deficit', which prevents effective multilateralism, a multilateralism that is based on a democratically evolved global consensus. Therefore, reform and restructuring of the United Nations system can alone provide a crucial link in an expanding chain of efforts to refashion international structures, imbuing them with a greater degree of participatory decision-making, so as to make them more representative of contemporary realities.

Our Millennium Declaration had recognised the urgency of the reform of the United Nations Security Council. An overwhelming majority of the world's population cannot be excluded from an institution that today legislates on an increasing number of issues, with an ever-widening impact. The expansion of the Security Council, in the category of both permanent and non-permanent members, and the inclusion of countries like India, as permanent members, would be a first step in the process of making the United Nations a truly representative body.

I would like to make brief references to two

countries with which India has had historically friendly ties and whose early return to political normalcy is the focus of the world's attention.

The situation in Iraq causes us great concern. The United Nations has a central role to play in erasing the discord of the recent past and in ensuring that the Iraqi people can soon exercise effective sovereignty, preserving the country's unity and territorial integrity. An end to the suffering of the Iraqi people and recognition of their aspirations should be the guiding objectives. Consistent with our long-standing ties of friendship with the Iraqi people, India will contribute to Iraq's humanitarian and economic reconstruction.

In the past three years, the international community has assisted Afghanistan in pulling back from the brink of chaos and chronic instability. We sincerely hope that the forthcoming Presidential elections and the subsequent Parliamentary elections will allow the Afghan people to express their will, free from interference and intimidation. India's assistance to Afghanistan's reconstruction and development will continue.

Relations between India and Pakistan have been a matter of attention for the international community. It is known that since January this year, India and Pakistan have initiated a composite dialogue to resolve all issues, including Jammu and Kashmir. I reaffirm our determination to carry forward this dialogue to a purposeful and mutually acceptable conclusion.

In closing Mr. President, I would like to reaffirm India's commitment to the principles that have brought us together in this Organisation.

These principles retain their relevance and validity even while the global economy and the international political order pose new and very different challenges. All of us have to grow out of the comfort of the predictable, discard constraining habits of thought and move forwards with confidence to meet the demands of the present and the future. Each of us has to be prepared to take on new obligations and larger responsibilities relevant to the needs of our times.

I deem it a privilege to say unhesitatingly that India is conscious of the responsibilities that lie ahead. I speak of an India on the move, on the cutting edge of economic, technological and developmental transformation. This is an India endowed with outstanding human resources, and we are putting in place policies, which will respond to emerging and critical tasks. We have the capability and the capacity to take these on, and to participate in the restructuring of a just and dynamic world order.

We are confident that in an inextricably interdependent world that we live in, our commitment to the common good, which this organisation embodies, will be resolute and firm.

In this, we are inspired by the vision of internationalism bequeathed to us by India's first Prime Minister – the great Jawaharlal Nehru – his vision of a world order whose pillars are peace, harmony, co-operation and development. This vision needs to reanimate the collective wisdom of the world community for a new partnership to meet the unprecedented challenges we face."

PM'S FAREWELL SPEECH TO THE 15TH LOK SABHA, FEBRUARY 21, 2014, NEW DELHI

"Madam Speaker,

As we come to the end of the journey of the fifteenth Lok Sabha, I join all the members of this August House in paying tribute to the way you have conducted our proceedings.

Madam,

In Parliamentary life, there are bound to be differences among parties, but there must also be ways and means of finding pathways to bring minimum amount of consistency and reconciliation, so that the ship of the Indian state can move forward. And we have seen that on certain crucial matters, this House has the capacity, the will to rise above partisan strife, and to find pathways of national reconciliation. The manner in which the way the state of Telangana is being born, is yet another indication that this country is capable of taking some of the most difficult decisions, without any rancour, without worrying too much about the pros and cons of things that do not matter, and we can take pride in the fact that Telangana state, whose quest for being born was pending for the last 60 years, has ultimately seen the light of day.

Food Security Bill is yet another landmark legislation. It will create a ray of hope among deprived sections of our community. It will provide a ray of hope to encourage our farmers to produce more. Sharad ji has described the manner in which the agricultural situation in our country has improved. And I compliment him on the manner in which he has guided the destiny of the Agriculture Ministry. Obviously, all members of the House have played a very important role in bringing that outcome about.

Madam,

We are now entering a phase where the people of India will once again have an opportunity to assess, to pass their judgement on the performance of Government, weaknesses of our Government, achievements of the Government, and it is in that process that once again, a new sense of consensus will emerge which will carry our country to new pathways.

I thank all Honourable Members of the House. I thank the Leader of the Opposition. I thank Shinde ji, who as Leader of the House has performed his duties with superb aplomb, and I wish all members of this August House the best. Let us hope that out of this strife, out of this tension-filled atmosphere which prevailed some times, there will be birth of a new atmosphere of hope.

With these words, I conclude my remarks by once again complimenting you for the manner, the grace in which you have conducting our proceedings."

NARENDRA MODI

SHRI NARENDRA DAMODARDAS MODI is the 15th and current Prime Minister of India, in office since May 2014. Modi, a leader of the Bharatiya Janata Party (BJP), previously served as the Chief Minister of Gujarat state from 2001 to 2014. He is currently the Member of Parliament (MP) from Varanasi.

On 13 October 2018, Modi was renamed as the BJP candidate for prime minister for the 2019 general election. After the Bharatiya Janata Party led National Democratic Alliance won a landslide in the 2014 Lok Sabha election, Narendra Modi was sworn in as the Prime Minister of India on 26 May 2014.

As of June 2024, Narendra Modi is serving his third term as the Prime Minister of India. His continued leadership reflects his enduring popularity and the electoral success of the Bharatiya Janata Party (BJP). In the 2024 general elections, the BJP once again secured a significant mandate, reflecting public confidence in Modi's leadership. Narendra Modi's third term as Prime Minister underscores his enduring influence in Indian politics.

Narendra Modi was born on 17 September 1950 to a family of grocers in Vadnagar, Mehsana district, in Bombay State (present-day Gujarat).

His family belonged to the Ghanchi (oil-presser) community, which is categorised among the other backward classes by the Indian government. He was the third of six children born to Damodardas Mulchand and Heeraben Modi. As a child, he helped his father Damodardas sell tea at the Vadnagar railway station, and later ran a tea stall with his brother near a bus terminus.

He completed his schooling in Vadnagar in 1967, where a teacher described him as being an average student, but a keen debater with an interest in theatre.

An early gift for rhetoric in debates was noted by teachers and students at the time. Modi also showed a preference for playing larger than life characters in theatre performances which has influenced the image he portrays of himself in politics. At the age of eight, Modi came into contact with the Rashtriya Swayamsevak Sangh (RSS) and began attending its local shakhas, or training sessions. There he met Lakshmanrao Inamdar, popularly known as Vakil Saheb, who was to become Modi's political mentor. Inamdar inducted Modi as a balswayamsevak, or junior cadet in the RSS.While training with the RSS, he also met Vasant Gajendragadkar and Nathalal Jaghda, Bharatiya Jana Sangh leaders who were later founding members of the BJP's Gujarat unit in 1980.

In keeping with the traditions of the Ghanchi caste, Modi's marriage was arranged by his parents while he was still a child. He was engaged at the age of 13 to Jashodaben Chimanlal, and married when he was 18. They spent little time together, and were soon estranged when Modi decided to pursue an itinerant life.

The marriage was reportedly never consummated. Modi kept the marriage secret for most of his career, only acknowledging the existence of his wife when filing his nomination for a parliamentary seat in the 2014 general elections.

Little is known of the time he spent traveling; however, in interviews Modi has spoken of visiting various Hindu ashrams, or places of Hindu religious learning, founded by Swami Vivekananda. The first of these was the Belur Math near Kolkata. He later visited the Advaita Ashrama in Almora, and the Ramakrishna mission in Rajkot. However he was only able to stay for a short period in each ashram, as he lacked a college education, and the institutions were strictly limited to postgraduates.

After two years of travel, Modi returned to Vadnagar, and after a brief visit left again for Ahmedabad. Here he lived with his uncle and worked at a canteen also run by his uncle at the Gujarat State Road Transport Corporation.

In Ahmedabad, Modi renewed his acquaintance with Inamdar, who was then based at Hedgewar Bhavan, the RSS headquarters in the city. After the end of the Indo-Pakistani War of 1971, he stopped working for his uncle and became a full–time pracharak (campaigner) of the RSS.

In 1978, Modi became a sambhaag pracharak (regional organiser) for the RSS, and also earned an extramural degree in political science through a distance education course at Delhi University. In 1983, he completed his Master of Arts degree in political science from Gujarat University.

On 26 June 1975, Prime Minister Indira Gandhi declared a unilateral state of emergency throughout the country, which lasted until 1977. During this period, many of her political opponents were jailed, and organisations opposing her, including the RSS, were banned. At the time, Modi was the pracharak in-charge of the Akhil Bharatiya Vidyarthi Parishad (ABVP), the student wing of the RSS. He was forced to go underground in Gujarat, and frequently traveled in disguise to avoid being arrested.

He became involved in printing booklets against the central government and distributing them to Delhi, as well as organising agitations. During this period, he also wrote a book in Gujarati titled Sangharsh ma Gujarat (The struggles of Gujarat) which described events during the emergency.

The RSS assigned Modi to the BJP in 1985. In 1988, Modi was elected an organising secretary of BJP's Gujarat unit, marking his formal entry into electoral politics. He rose to prominence within the party after helping organise L. K. Advani's Ayodhya Rath Yatra in 1990 and Murli Manohar

Joshi's Ekta Yatra (Journey for Unity) in 1991–92.

His electoral strategy as secretary was seen to be central to the BJP's victory in the 1995 state assembly elections. Later in the same year in November, Modi was elected National Secretary of the BJP, and was transferred to New Delhi where he was assigned responsibility for the party's activities in Haryana and Himachal Pradesh. In 1996, Shankersinh Vaghela, one of the most prominent leaders of the BJP in Gujarat, defected to the INC after he lost his parliamentary seat in the 1996 Lok Sabha elections. While on the selection committee for the 1998 Assembly elections in Gujarat, Modi favoured supporters of Patel over those loyal to Vaghela, in an attempt to put an end to the factional divisions within the party. His strategies were credited as being key to the BJP winning an overall majority in the 1998 elections. As a result, Modi was promoted to the post of general secretary (Organisation) of the BJP in May 1998.

In 2001, Keshubhai Patel's health was failing, and the BJP had lost seats in the by-elections. Allegations of abuse of power, corruption and poor administration were being made, and Patel's standing had been damaged by his administration's handling of the Bhuj Earthquake of 2001. As a result, the BJP's national leadership sought a new candidate for the office of chief minister, and Modi, who had aired his misgivings about Patel's administration, was chosen as a replacement. L. K. Advani, a senior leader of the BJP, did not want to ostracise Patel and was worried about Modi's lack of experience in governance. Modi declined an offer to be Patel's deputy chief minister, informing Advani and Atal Bihari Vajpayee that he was "going to be fully responsible for Gujarat or not at all", and on 3 October 2001, Modi was named as the replacement of Patel as the Chief Minister of

Gujarat, with the responsibility of preparing the BJP for elections in December 2002. As Chief Minister, Modi's ideas of governance revolved around privatisation and small government, which stood at odds with what political commentator Aditi Phadnis has described as the anti-privatisation, anti-globalisation position of the RSS.

Narendra Modi was sworn in as Prime Minister on 26 May 2014 at the Rastrapati Bhavan. He is India's first prime minister born after the country's independence. In a first of its kind, Modi invited all SAARC leaders to attend his swearing-in ceremony; the attendees included Afghanistan President Hamid Karzai, Sri Lankan President Mahinda Rajapaksa, Bhutan Prime Minister Tshering Tobgay, Maldives President Abdulla Yameen Abdul Gayoom, Prime Minister Navin Ramgoolam of Mauritius (SAARC observer), Nepal Prime Minister Sushil Koirala, Prime Minister of Pakistan Nawaz Sharif, and Speaker of the National Parliament of Bangladesh Shirin Sharmin Chaudhury. Bangladesh Prime Minister Sheikh Hasina could not attend since she had a scheduled state visit to Japan and deputed the Speaker of National Parliament of Bangladesh to attend the ceremony on her behalf.

Modi's first cabinet consisted of 45 ministers, less than the 70 ministers of the previous government. Modi invited the leaders of SAARC countries to his swearing-in ceremony for taking office as Prime Minister, to strengthen the diplomatic relationship and increase business. Continuing with the aim of promoting close ties with neighbouring countries, Modi's first foreign visit as Prime Minister of India was to Bhutan . He later visited Nepal on August 8, 2014.[182][183] Later, he made a 5 day bilateral visit to Japan starting on August 30, 2014.

On 17 September 2014, Chinese President Xi Jinping arrived

in India and several FINANCIAL MoUs and agreements of cooperation were signed between the two countries. which Modi termed as a new chapter in the economic relations of both them.[186] Modi visited the United States in the last week of September 2014, which was described as very successful, leading to a boosting of bilateral relations between India and the US.

Modi is a vegetarian. He has a frugal lifestyle, is a workaholic and an introvert. He writes poems in Gujarati. As a speaker, he is known as a crowd-puller. In the critical opinion of Somini Sengupta, writing for The New York Times in a 2009 article on the Supreme Court's ordering of an investigation into Modi's role in the 2002 Gujarat riots, "Mr. Modi has assiduously sought to reinvent himself from a scruffy mascot of Hindu nationalism to a decisive corporate-style administrator".

He emerged as social media savvy politician and since September 2014 is the second most followed leader in the world with over 6 million followers on Twitter. His interaction on Google Hangouts on 31 August 2012 made Modi the first Indian politician to interact with netizens through live chat on the internet.

Modi has been labelled by the media and some articles in peer-reviewed journals as a controversial, polarising and divisive figure, but British economist Jim O'Neill, author of the BRIC report, wrote on his blog that Modi is "good on economics", one of the things that "India desperately needs in a leader".

In August 2013, FINANCIAL analyst Chris Wood, chief strategist of CLSA, wrote in his weekly Greed & Fear that "the INDIAN STOCK MARKET'S greatest hope is the emergence of Gujarat Chief Minister Narendra Modi as the BJP's prime ministerial candidate".

In March 2012 and June 2014, Modi appeared on the cover of the Asian edition of Time Magazine, one of the few Indian politicians to have done so. He was awarded Indian of the Year by CNN-News18 (formally CNN-IBN) news network in 2014.

In June 2015, Modi was featured on the cover of Time Magazine. In 2014, 2015, 2017, 2020 and 2021, he was named one of Time magazine's 100 Most Influential People in the World. Forbes Magazine ranked him the 15th Most Powerful Person in the World in 2014 and the 9th Most Powerful Person in the World in 2015, 2016 and 2018.

In 2015, Modi was ranked the 13th Most Influential Person in the World by Bloomberg Markets Magazine. Modi was ranked fifth on Fortune Magazine's first annual list of the "World's Greatest Leaders" in 2015.

In 2017, Gallup International Association (GIA) conducted a poll and ranked Modi as third top leader of the world.

In 2016, a wax statue of Modi was unveiled at Madame Tussauds wax museum in London.

In 2018, he was the third most followed world leader on Twitter, and the most followed world leader on Facebook and Instagram. In October 2018, Modi received United Nations's highest environmental award, the 'Champions of the Earth', for policy leadership by "pioneering work in championing" the International Solar Alliance and "new areas of levels of cooperation on environmental action".

The Texas India Forum hosted a community event in honour of Modi on 22 September 2019 at the NRG Stadium in Houston, Texas.

He was awarded the Global Goalkeeper Award on 24 September 2019 in New York City by the Bill & Melinda Gates Foundation in recognition for the Swachh Bharat Mission and "the progress India has made in providing safe sanitation under his leadership".

In 2020, Modi was among eight world leaders awarded the parodic Ig Nobel Prize in Medical Education "for using the COVID-19 viral pandemic to teach the world that politicians can have a more immediate effect on life and death than scientists and doctors can".

On 21 December 2020, President Donald Trump awarded Modi with the Legion of Merit for elevating the India–United States relations. The Legion of Merit was awarded to Modi along with Prime Minister of Australia Scott Morrison and former Prime Minister of Japan Shinzo Abe, the "original architects" of the QUAD.

On 24 February 2021, the largest cricket stadium in the world at Ahmedabad was renamed Narendra Modi Stadium by the Gujarat Cricket Association.

Modi is featured in TIME Magazine's 100 most influential people of 2021 list, making it his fifth time after 2014, 2015, 2017, and 2020. TIME called him the third "pivotal leader" of independent India after Jawaharlal Nehru and Indira Gandhi who "dominated the country's politics like no one since them".

~~~
~~~